One for Silver, Two for Gold

Mary May

BOOKS IN THIS SERIES

The Will to Win
Piebald is Lucky
Deep Water at Dereen
One for Silver, Two for Gold

Also

A Patchwork of Ponies
(A collection of short stories)

One for Silver, Two for Gold

by

Mary May

Cover Design by Gregory Larcombe
from the illustrations
by
Anne Grahame Johnstone

British Library Cataloguing-in-publication data
A CIP catalogue record for this book is available
from the British Library

Printed and bound in the UK
by Antony Rowe Ltd.

Published by

ISBN 09526838 4 9

DEDICATION

Anne Grahame Johnstone's artistry has created enchanting colour covers and delightful black and white illustrations which have brought all my books to life. Anne has always given me encouragement and support, but most of all she has become a real friend. It is to Anne that I dedicate this book with my thanks and love.

Anne lost her battle against liver cancer, which she fought with such courage and dignity, on May 25th 1997.

FOREWORD

What fun to read a childrens book that covers a subject so dear to my heart. The enchanting detail of the trials and tribulations of learning to drive a pony pair, the fixes the children get in, their problem solving and their achievements a reflection of the fun that can be had whilst driving ponies. As a child I dreamed of owning my very own pony and I wish that this book had been written then as it would have enabled me to learn earlier about the sport of carriage driving. It makes pair driving sound so much fun whilst not ignoring some of the difficulties! It could well fuel the ambitions of carriage drivers for the future.

Clare Weigrove

PREFACE

This is a very special preface. Anne Grahame Johnstone, who has illustrated all my books and to whom I have dedicated this book, lost her fight against liver cancer in May this year. Anne was working on commissions until just before she died, but despite enormous courage and hard work she had been unable to do the illustrations for One for Silver, Two for Gold.

I would like to thank her brother, Murray, for his generosity in giving me permission on this one occasion to use illustrations Anne had done for me before, so that this book could have pictures too.

I am extremely grateful to Clare Wigmore L.H.H.I. Despite a very busy life Clare found time not only to write the foreword to this book, but also to check the text, particularly the parts concerning pair driving where she is very experienced and I am not!

I would also like to thank my family and William Thwaite for their support throughout this book, especially my son-in-law, Gregory Larcombe, for his sensitive use of Anne's illustrations to create the colour cover and the black and white pictures.

Chapter I

The small piebald pony plodded diligently round on the lunge. Carol watched from her wheelchair by the gate of the field. The sun was shining, and a pair of hedge sparrows were busy flying in and out of the hawthorn hedge with beaks full of twigs. It was a beautiful day in late spring.

Oh dear, Carol thought, how awful, he's just too quiet and too good. She sighed. After the wonderful holiday, full of adventure, that she and her friends had just enjoyed in Ireland over the Easter holidays, the gift of Paddy, the little piebald pony, had seemed like a dream come true.

Carol had been disabled in a car accident over two years ago. Her beloved show pony had been sold, and she had been devastated. Since then Carol had fought to return to as near normal a life as possible. It had not been easy to accept that she would never walk without crutches, or ride to show standard again. Instead, with the help of her very good friends, Liz and Patsy, she had taken up carriage driving, where no one could see her useless legs.

Liz had started to teach her to drive with her pony, Harmony. Liz and Harmony were already a winning combination, driving at many local shows. It was by chance they had discovered that Pinto, the fat, shaggy piebald pony that belonged to Patsy, Carol's other great friend, was also a driving pony. Patsy's father was the local vicar, and he and her mother knew very little about ponies. So Pinto had moved half a mile up the road to Carol's home. Carol's parents, Mr and Mrs. Lane, had show experience and expertise. Carol had driven Pinto and Patsy had acted as her groom. They had had a lot of fun. Carol loved Pinto dearly, but, he wasn't hers either.

Then she had been given Paddy, who was as like Pinto as two peas are in a pod. Her very own pony at last. Carol had been so excited and had made plans to drive, not only Paddy, but Paddy and Pinto as a pair.

Now, instead of being thrilled and excited, she was feeling guilty because she was disappointed. Carol watched her mother gloomily. Her parents were the ones who were thrilled.

1

Her mother called "Whoa" and Paddy obediently stopped. Mrs. Lane collected up the lunge line and walked him over to the gate, her face wreathed in smiles.

"He's so good, Carol!" she exclaimed, "I know he hasn't the charisma of Harmony or the perkiness of Pinto, but he is going to be 100% obedient and safe. I can't believe that you have been lucky enough to be given such a suitable pony."

"He's certainly very docile and obedient." Carol agreed, stretching out her hand to caress the little pony. He whickered softly, and she felt even more ashamed of herself. He was sweet. She was lucky. Yet she knew deep down she was disappointed. He wouldn't be a challenge.

Her mother was delighted. She and Mr Lane were carefully going through all the schooling necessary for a driving pony to find out what he knew. They decided that he probably hadn't been long reined before, because he had stood looking very bewildered, wondering why the commands were coming from behind him. However he had willingly and quickly learnt this new accomplishment. When Mrs. Roberts, who was Liz's mother and an experienced whip, had come to drive Paddy for the first time, Paddy had stood like a lamb. Mrs. Roberts had taken him round the field, and as he was being so good, she had driven him down the lane towards the village and back along the small lane behind the house. He hadn't put a foot wrong. They had all been so pleased. Liz, who had gone as backstep groom for her mother, thought he was going to be super.

Mrs. Lane undid the lunging cavesson, and turned the little pony out in the field. He wandered slowly across to Pinto, but stopped half way and pawed at the ground.

"He's going to roll," Carol laughed, "after all the work I put in from my wheelchair cleaning the mud off before you worked him!

As Carol and her mother turned to go back to the stables they stopped, and turned, listening. Carol's mother looked back down the drive which ran alongside the ponies' paddock to the road.

"Did I hear a horse trotting?" she queried.

"Oh look!" Carol exclaimed, "it's Liz, Mrs. Roberts and Harmony."

"Hi," Liz called, as she drove Harmony up the gravel drive towards them. "We didn't bother to 'phone. It's such a lovely day

2

and we need to get Harmony fit, so we got the exercise cart out and thought we'd come over to see you. If you'd been out we would have just gone through the village, and back the other way."

"Hallo, Liz," Mrs. Lane smiled at the tall slim girl, who was a year older than Carol, then she walked across to talk to Liz's mother who was getting down to go and hold Harmony.

"Have we called at a bad time? Are you busy or could we beg a cup of tea?" Mrs. Roberts asked.

"We'd love to give you tea. Come and put Harmony in the stable and then we'll go across to the house."

"You don't need me with three of you to unharness Harmony," Carol said, "I'll go on ahead and put the kettle on." She wheeled her chair over, and reached up to pat Harmony's bay neck. "Hallo, old boy." She looked up at Liz, "See you in a minute." She grinned at her friend and continued on her way to the house. At the front door she stopped and reached for her crutches which she kept strapped on the chair. Then slowly she eased herself out of the chair, up onto her crutches and made her way to the kitchen. By the time the two mothers and Liz had joined her, she had laid the table and made a pot of tea. Carol had been using crutches for over two years now, and had learnt to be agile and competent in getting about. It was surprising how much she could achieve.

"Well, how is Paddy progressing?" Liz asked eagerly as she came into the kitchen.

"Fine," Carol looked at Liz, "he's as good as gold." Liz looked back at Carol curiously.

"But that's good, isn't it?" she queried, "you sound a bit flat."

"Yes, it's good," Carol agreed rather unenthusiastically, "and I feel such an ungrateful pig, but he is almost too quiet. Mummy and Daddy are delighted because they feel he is so safe for me. Still I suppose it means he's ideal to try and make a pair with Pinto. I think that is really exciting, and if Paddy had been at all difficult, driving a pair would have been vetoed."

"How are you going to learn to drive a pair?" Liz asked, "have you thought about it?"

"Not really," Carol admitted, "we've been too busy finding out how much Paddy really does know."

"One of the reasons I wanted to drive over today was to ask

3

you about dates for your half term, and show you this." Liz waved a piece of paper at Carol, "it's details of a junior whip camp at a carriage driving centre about forty miles away. It's run over my half term, and I'm really keen to go. I thought you and Patsy might have come too. It should be great fun. Maybe you could learn to drive a pair, they might teach you there."

"Oh, Liz, that would be super," Carol looked up hopefully, and then her face fell. "I don't think it will be any good though, because you get a whole week home from boarding school. Patsy and I only get the Friday and Monday." They looked at the dates. "Bother," Carol said sadly, "just as I thought. I don't expect we'd be allowed to come for just the last three days."

"I could find out," Liz replied, "but it doesn't sound very hopeful. What a shame, still I think there is a second camp in the summer hols, perhaps you could go to that."

"Will you go to both? Carol asked.

"I'm not sure," Liz looked down at the paper, "I think it will depend on what the first camp is like. If I feel I'm really learning a lot I could use the bursary I won at the show last year to go a second time."

"What sort of things go on at camp?" Carol was eager to know.

"There's instruction, demonstrations, lectures, drives, competitions, a barbecue and we have a chance to take the B.D.S. grade exams."

"Would you want to take any exams? We get enough of those at school."

"I think I might like to. It would be useful to make sure one knew the correct way to do things. It's so easy not to bother to do things properly. I thought I'd get copy of the syllabus from the B.D.S. and see what is involved. It's a bit of a challenge too, something to work for during the week."

"I'd like to have a look when you get a copy. I wonder how difficult the first exam is?"

"I shouldn't think it would be very hard, I imagine the idea is to encourage people to start with, rather like the D test at Pony Club."

Mrs. Lane leaned across the table towards the girls. "Shall we harness Pinto, Carol, and drive some of the way back with Liz and

4

Mrs. Roberts? I think I could be a substitute groom for Patsy by now, couldn't I?"

"Oh, yes, that would be fun. Patsy's gone shopping with her mother for boring clothes and shoes for school, so I didn't think I'd get a drive today." Carol's face lit up. "We could go about half way and then turn off to come home along the back lane."

"You are getting brave!" Mrs. Roberts laughed at Carol's mother. "It's not all that long ago we had to bully you to get in a vehicle with your daughter."

They all set too and cleared away the tea things before going back to the stables. Liz helped Carol and her mother catch and harness Pinto while Mrs. Roberts harnessed Harmony. Then the two ponies were put to their exercise carts. Mrs. Roberts got in to drive Harmony while Carol clambered up behind Pinto. Their grooms got up to join them and the little procession set off.

Already Harmony and Pinto had lost their woolly winter coats and were in shiny summer condition. Both Liz and Carol had made plans to enter the Royal Windsor Horse Show in May. There was quite friendly but keen rivalry to get their ponies fit and in good condition early. The year before Carol and Patsy hadn't been ready to take Carol's lovely show phaeton to Windsor, and they had contented themselves with entering a road safety competition. This year they were going to compete with the phaeton for the first time.

"Would you let me go to a junior driving camp this summer?" Carol asked her mother as they trotted along following Harmony.

"I should think so, Mrs. Roberts says Liz is very keen, and that the camps are both fun and instructional. I understand you won't be able to go to the same camp as Liz at half term, but apparently there is another in the summer holidays."

"I wouldn't be able to go unless Patsy came too. I'd never manage on my own, but I think Patsy would probably think it was jolly good fun." Carol eased Pinto back to a walk as they approached a T junction. "Our paths part here," she waved as Liz and Mrs. Roberts turned right to drive back to Blakewell Forest. As Harmony trotted off the others waved back. Carol turned left and Pinto quickened his stride, knowing he was going home.

"Are you enjoying yourself, Mummy?" Carol glanced sideways at her mother.

"I really am, Carol, I have a lot of confidence in you and Pinto. On a lovely day like this it is a super way to travel. I'm not sure I'd be so keen when it's cold and wet though." They lapsed into a companionable silence until they reached home. Carol drove Pinto through the village and up the lane past the rectory where Patsy lived. Half a mile further on they turned into the drive of Old Chimneys. "Home again," Carol said happily, "that was unexpected, but great fun. I'll allow you to be my groom again when Patsy can't come!"

"That is high praise." Her mother smiled, and got down to hold Pinto's head. Carol clambered down and reached for her crutches.

"Pinto's so good, Mummy, that I can balance on my crutches and hold him. If you could undo the breeching, bellyband and the traces, then you can push the cart back." Between them they managed, and Mrs. Lane led Pinto back from the stables to the field where Paddy was waiting for him by the gate.

CHAPTER II

"Are we going driving?" Patsy called across to Carol as she skidded to a halt on the gravel drive.

"Hi." Carol looked very full of herself. Patsy propped her bike against the stable wall. Her arms were already tanned brown. She had on her usual pair of faded denim jeans and trainers. She always managed to look untidy, her hair was windswept and her tee-shirt had grease on it.

"Sorry I'm a bit late, the chain came off my bike."

"Bad luck," Carol dismissed the chain and bike as unimportant. "Guess what? Mummy's going shopping, but we can drive Paddy in the field." Patsy's face fell.

"Not more schooling," she said, "I'm getting bored with all this paddock work. Paddy's dead quiet. Why won't your parents let us take him out for a proper drive?"

"I think they will soon, but I've had a great idea. Let's put a cone course up and pretend we're scurry driving."

"Wow! You're mother won't like that, will she?" Patsy looked startled. "It's not exactly schooling, is it?"

"We'll wait until she's gone shopping. We can go and get him ready, then, when we see her drive off, we'll put the cones out."

"You mean I'll have to," Patsy groaned in mock horror, "slaving for you again."

"Stop moaning, it'll be fun. I wonder if we can get him to canter round?" The two girls moved towards the stables. Patsy collected a headcollar and went to catch Paddy, while Carol fetched the grooming kit.

"He's still moulting." Patsy complained, trying to brush the white hairs off her shirt. "These hairs have stuck on the bike grease. Mum will be cross, this was clean on this morning."

"He's beginning to look good though, isn't he? He's nearly as smart as Pinto and Harmony," Carol looked round, "he had such a thick coat when he first arrived, but I expect he lived out all year round in Ireland." Patsy put her brush down and went to fetch the harness.

"It's a good job he and Pinto are the same size, and Pinto's harness fits him," she said as she came back with a pile of harness.

Carol heard the car engine start up.

"Listen. Mother's going, we can go and put the cones out." Patsy put down the breast collar she was holding.

"O.K. We'll come back and harness up in a minute."

It took longer than they expected to make a course, even with Carol carrying some of the cones on her wheel chair.

"We'd better leave plenty of space between the pairs of cones to start with," Carol called, "I want to see if we can canter Paddy round."

"You'll have to walk and trot first, won't you?" Patsy rubbed a sticky hand across her face. "It's warm, isn't it?" The two girls made their way back to harness Paddy up and put him to the exercise cart.

It was rather a grey but muggy day. The hawthorn hedges around the fields were heavy with white blossom, and the smell of the flowers filled the air. Patsy opened the gate and Carol drove Paddy into the field. She hopped up on the back step and Carol walked him round. Paddy was his usual obedient and rather uninspired self, as they wove in and out of the cones to see how the distances felt.

"Oh, this is boring!" Carol exclaimed, "let's try a bit faster. Paddy, trot on." The little pony trotted round. There were two pairs of cones set rather close to either side of a bend, and the distances were quite tight at the trot. There was plenty of space everywhere else. As they passed the last cones Carol flicked Paddy with the whip.

"Come on, Paddy. Canter!" she encouraged as they headed for their finish line. The exercise cart bounced over the grass and Patsy hung onto the rail at the back. "That was more fun, wasn't it?" she glanced at Patsy on the backstep as she slowed him back to trot again. "Shall we try the whole course at canter?"

"Why not?" Patsy grinned, "I'll have to hang on tight." They set off for the first pair of cones, Paddy cantering steadily.

"Help, it's not so easy!" Carol gasped, the cones seemed to come up very quickly. There was a crunch as the left hand wheel knocked a cone flying. She tried to correct the turn by turning her wrists and looping the rein but she wasn't quick enough and the next pair of cones went flying too. The exercise cart tilted as it ran over the fallen cones and the sudden lurch caused Patsy to lose her balance. The next moment she lay sprawled in the grass while Carol and Paddy cantered away through the finish.

Patsy picked herself up and looked across to see if Carol was all right. She was relieved to see her bringing Paddy back to a walk.

"Are you O.K.?" Carol turned the vehicle round and started back towards Patsy. "What happened?" she went on.

"I wasn't expecting the lurch over the cones," Patsy replied, standing the offending cone back up. "I just completely lost my grip and fell, but I'm fine. I haven't hurt myself at all."

"We didn't do very well, did we?" Carol pulled Paddy up. "Do you think we should move the cones a bit further apart before we have another go?" Patsy nodded, and adjusted their position.

"How about that?" she queried, "does that look better?"

"We'll soon find out. For heavens sake hold on tightly this time." Patsy ran up behind to jump back onto the back step as Carol moved Paddy off again.

"Well, don't take off without warning me," she said breathlessly as she swung herself up. The sun started to break through the clouds, and it began to feel very hot. The perspiration was running down Patsy's face.

Carol found it easier with the extra spacing, but her reins seemed too long and she didn't have time at canter to shorten them.

"I'm sure we're not doing this quite right," she exclaimed as once more a cone bit the dust.

"What do you mean 'we'? I'm only hanging on behind, you're the one whose meant to be in control!" Patsy cried indignantly, remembering to grip tightly as Carol pushed Paddy flat out through the finish. "Anyway, that was much better, you only just tipped that last cone, you were a bit unlucky it fell." She jumped down and went to Paddy's head. "Poor Paddy, he's puffing like mad. He's not nearly as fit as Pinto."

"Help! We'd better walk him to cool him off, and call it a day." Carol felt rather guilty. She'd been enjoying herself, and they had pushed Paddy rather hard. "I wonder where we could find out more about scurrying, because it is fun, isn't it?"

"P'raps Liz will know, and if she doesn't I expect her mother will." Patsy walked at Paddy's head as they went back to the stable yard.

"If we have another go next time Mummy goes out, we ought to have a stop watch and time each round." Carol said thoughtfully. Chatting happily the girls dealt with the little pony, put the harness away and turned him out.

"You hold your reins one in each hand for scurry driving." Liz told Carol on the telephone later that day. "It gives you more control at speed. Haven't you seen them at shows, or watched scurry on TV? They have special, lightweight, four wheel vehicles as well. You're meant to sit with your feet braced and your body leaning forward to reduce wind resistance and make you more streamlined, like a racing car."

"Patsy said you'd know all about it. Have you ever had a go?" Carol queried.

"No, but it does look fun. I've watched at one or two shows where there has been a scurry competition." Liz explained, "Are you thinking of scurrying Paddy and Pinto? I'm not sure your parents would think much of that idea."

"I don't know really. It was just something to liven Paddy up. I suppose I'd better learn to drive a pair first."

"I'm off to junior whip camp next week," Liz added, "then

almost immediately after that it will be the Windsor Horse Show. Mother will keep Harmony exercised while I'm away. It should be fun at camp, but I wish you and Patsy were coming too."

"So do I, but we're hoping to go to the next one in the summer hols. Mummy's got all the details. We decided we'd wait and see what you thought before we committed ourselves."

The girls didn't have the chance to practise scurry driving for some days. The evenings were getting lighter, and most nights after school Patsy, Carol and her mother worked the ponies. Pinto got most attention as he had to be fit and looking immaculate for Windsor. They were all getting quite excited.

It seemed strange with Liz away. Although she lived eight miles away, and went to boarding school, the three girls kept in touch almost daily.

"I hope she's having a good time." Patsy was polishing the brass buckles on the harness as they cleaned it after the evening practice. "I expect she's doing lots of tack cleaning too."

"Roll on Friday and half term." Carol said with feeling.

"Yes, but we shall mess up all this beautifully cleaned tack," Patsy said sadly, looking at the clean pile of harness with satisfaction. "I've finished my half, I'll start putting it back together."

The two girls had spent a lot of time driving Pinto with the show phaeton. They were only allowed to use it in the run up to a big show, and preferably on dry days, so it kept fairly clean.

"It's fun taking the phaeton on the road." Patsy said happily. "I feel rather grand, because it's so smart, and people stop and stare or wave."

"As if we're Royalty!" Carol grinned, "you're a real show off, Patsy, but I know what you mean, it is rather special!"

Mrs. Lane came into the harness room. "Oh, good, you've nearly finished. I thought I'd come and find you. Mrs. Roberts has just 'phoned to say that on Sunday, the last day at the junior whip camp, the children put on a display and a fun competition. She wondered if you'd like to go and watch."

Patsy turned round excitedly. She was hanging the harness back on its hooks on the wall. "That would be great, wouldn't it, Carol?"

"Yes, we could see what it's like, and ask about the summer

camp." Carol flicked her fair hair behind her with a hand that was sticky with saddle soap.

"You check with your mother, Patsy, and if she's happy, I'll take you both and we'll have a picnic." Mrs. Lane smiled at the girls. "It will be interesting to see a driving centre and fun to see how Liz has got on." She helped them put away the rest of the clean harness, and then the three of them made their way back to the house. It was a warm May evening and the large creamy white elderflowers were hanging heavy on the branches of the bushes, their delicate smell mingling with the garden flowers to make the evening air seem gently scented.

Patsy stopped by her bike. "Back home to history prep," she said with a resigned air, "see you in the morning." She waved as she pedalled down the road towards the vicarage.

The front door of the house stood open. Pip and Squeak, the two Jack Russell terriers, were still lying on the lawn. As Carol negotiated her wheelchair inside they got up together and followed her into the house.

"Did you have a good drive?" Mr. Lane called from the kitchen as he heard them come in.

"They're looking rather good." Mrs. Lane answered. Carol laughed.

"I think Pinto is going as well as he ever has. I just hope we can put on a super performance at Windsor."

CHAPTER III

Sunday had ended in disaster. Late that evening Carol lay tossing in her bed, chasing elusive sleep. She still couldn't believe what had happened. To start with they had enjoyed a lovely day. Liz had bubbled with enthusiasm and had been so pleased to see them.

"I've had such a super week," she told them excitedly, "it's been great fun, everyone has been so friendly. We've done all sorts of thing and I've learnt lots. You'll see later." She had turned to a tall, dark haired boy who stood beside her. "This is David. He and I have taken it in turns to groom for each other all week."

"Hi," David grinned at them, his face welcoming. "Liz and I have made a good team. Liz has told me all about you both, it will be great if you can come to the summer camp. We want to come back and team up again, don't we Liz?"

They had been a good pair. Carol turned over restlessly and pushed her duvet onto the floor. She was too hot, it was a very warm evening. Liz and David had won a competition. It had been a scurry competition around cones and Carol had to bite back feelings of envy as she watched them race round very competently. Patsy had been much nicer, she thought miserably to herself. "They'll be able to help us!" Patsy had said, eyes alight with enthusiasm. "Liz and David make it look so easy Carol, I'm sure they'll show us all the things they've been taught."

Carol had been surprised that she had minded. She had wanted to be the one who was good at scurry, and now Liz and her new friend could do it much better. What a beast she was to feel jealous. She had swallowed hard and joined in the congratulations.

She had been genuinely thrilled at the prize giving when Liz went up to collect her B.D.S. level one and two certificates. Then Liz and David had collected rosettes for the second best pair of the week. Carol felt unsure about David. She'd never had much to do with boys. Patsy's twin brothers were younger than Patsy and away at boarding school. In the holidays their interests were very different and their paths hardly ever crossed. David was older, Liz had said he was fourteen. Patsy had chattered away to him as she

13

did to everyone, but Carol felt suddenly very aware of her wheelchair and crutches.

The final bombshell had been the news from her mother that she didn't think they would take Carol at the summer camp.

"Why not, Mummy?" she had cried incredulously.

"Well darling, they have a special camp for disabled children and they think you would do better at that, where there are more helpers."

"I don't need special helpers. I've got Patsy," she'd cried rebelliously, "Patsy and I are just as good as any pair here. I'm not going to a disabled camp!"

"Don't make a fuss now," her mother looked sadly at Carol. "You'll spoil Liz and David's day. I'll try and talk to the camp organisers next week. They're busy at the moment, and it's the end of a tiring time for them. It's much better to hide your disappointment if you can."

No one had even noticed how quiet Carol had become. Liz and David were so elated. Patsy rushed about looking at everything, and Carol had felt very left out. It had been a job to smile. The rest of the day had been a nightmare.

On the way home in the car Patsy had been outraged when she realised Carol might be turned down for camp. Her fury had been immediate.

"It's stupid!" she had stormed angrily. "Carol's better than most of the people I've seen driving today."

"I know that," Mrs. Lane had said, "and you know that, but the camp organisers don't."

"We must tell them," Patsy had gone on, "I'm not going without Carol. I don't want to do the driving. I just enjoy being a groom. We're a team, aren't we Carol?"

Carol had felt better for Patsy's staunch support, but when she had finally got to bed, everything had closed in on her. I shall never be like them, she thought. I'm disabled and it creates a barrier with people. At school I'm accepted now for what I am, but every time I do something new it's my disability that is the first thing anyone knows about me. It was a long time before she got to sleep.

The 'phone rang early the next morning. It was Liz. "Can you and Patsy drive over to lunch?" she asked hopefully. "I don't have to go back to school until this evening, and you've got today off, haven't you?"

"Yes, we have," Carol agreed, I'll ring Patsy and find out, then I'll ring you back." She didn't really want to go but she knew Patsy loved the drive over to Liz's house and sure enough Patsy was delighted.

"I'll be over straight away," she cried.

"Bring a coat," Carol said, but Patsy had already put the 'phone down. She came tearing up the drive on her bike a few moments later. Between them Paddy was caught, groomed, harnessed up and put to the exercise cart. "I think we should take coats," Carol turned to Patsy, "I tried to tell you to bring yours when I 'phoned, but you'd gone." Patsy looked up at the sky.

"It is a bit grey," she agreed, "Have you an old anorak I can borrow?"

"You know I have!" Carol picked up two coats and put them in the cart. "I brought my old one for you. I guessed you wouldn't bring one with you."

"Thanks." Patsy moved to Paddy's head as Carol got in. Then as Paddy moved off she came round and scrambled up beside Carol. She looked across at her friend. Carol is rather quiet, she thought, I don't think I'll mention camp before we reach the Robert's house.

The eight mile journey passed quite quickly. The way was so familiar now that it didn't seem so long. The girls had decided to make this Paddy's first long journey. He had been used more and more on short trips recently. It had amused Carol the first time she and Patsy had driven him to the village. Most people hadn't even noticed that it wasn't Pinto that she was driving. The only person who had noticed was old Mr. Wilkins at the post office. To Carol they looked quite different, but she supposed to most people one piebald pony was much like another. Pinto was super-fit because they worked him every evening, but Paddy was getting streamlined as well. The sixteen miles, eight each way, that they were driving today would be the most he'd done in one day. He trotted along willingly and steadily, taking no notice of the occasional car or lorry that passed. His black mane was still resisting all their efforts to keep it pulled and tidy, and was tossing about wildly. Pinto's mane had far more white in it and fell neatly on the off side.

"It's very relaxing driving Paddy," Carol looked at Patsy, "I think he's enjoying a longer outing."

"I know you're disappointed that he's not more lively," Patsy replied, "but he is a dear. He's so easy to handle, and after all you could always pep his feed up with some oats if you want him leaping about."

"I suppose I could," Carol was thoughtful, "I think I'd better let him get settled in first. While he's so quiet we can play with the cones and scurry driving."

It was almost twelve o'clock as they turned into the Roberts drive and there was a strange car parked near the back door.

"I wonder who that is? I don't recognise that car." Carol was just looking at the car when the back door opened, Liz, David, Mr. and Mrs. Roberts and another two adults came out. Carol's heart sank.

"Oh good," Patsy cried, "David's here, and I suppose those are his parents. Hi" she called, "We've had a super drive over, and it hasn't rained yet." As Carol pulled Paddy up, Patsy jumped out and went to the little pony's head. "Look!" she went on enthusiastically, "we've brought Paddy today, it's his first long outing."

The little group moved across to greet them. Carol felt even more awkward than usual climbing down from the cart. Liz went round to the back and unstrapped her crutches.

"Thanks." Carol said. She got herself on her crutches, took a deep breath, looked up and smiled. "Hallo again, David," she said bravely, "these must be your parents?"

"Yes, hi, Carol. Mother, Father, this is Carol and this is Patsy. This is Paddy because Patsy said so! The girls have two piebald ponies who are very alike. Patsy owns Paddy and Carol owns Pinto."

"Wrong!" Patsy and Liz called." Patsy owns Pinto and Carol owns Paddy!" They all laughed. David's mother and father came over.

"So you're Carol," David's father said, "we've heard such a lot about you, and how brilliantly you have done with your driving since your accident. I hear you even won an award at Olympia." Carol went scarlet.

16

"Oh dear, Liz," she said, "whatever have you been saying?"

"Only the truth." Liz laughed.

"And now you're going to be competition for Liz and David at the summer camp." David's mother said gaily. There was a sudden silence, and Carol looked embarrassed and upset. "What have I said?" Mrs. Templar asked. Patsy couldn't control herself any more.

"They won't take Carol at the summer camp," she burst out, "I think it's absolutely rotten." Liz looked stunned.

"Why not?" she said in amazement. Carol felt very awkward, then she looked defiantly at them all.

"Because I'm disabled, of course." There, she had said it, she took a deep breath. "They think I should go to a camp for disabled children where there will be more helpers. I have Patsy who is brilliant. We've always worked together, but I suppose they can't be expected to know that." Suddenly the tears threatened to spring up in her eyes, and she turned away. "Don't let's talk about it. What do you want us to do with Paddy?" Mrs. Roberts broke the uncomfortable silence.

"Why don't you take Paddy round and pop him into the stable while we have some lunch. Then we can talk about the afternoon afterwards." Carol held Paddy while Patsy undid the breeching, belly band and traces. She moved the exercise cart backwards. David made to move forward to help, but Liz put her hand out and shook her head warningly at him. Patsy led Paddy round and Carol followed on her crutches. Between them the girls soon had Paddy unharnessed and into the stable. It was quite obvious to the onlookers that each girl had their own tasks and Patsy knew exactly what Carol could and couldn't do.

"Let's go on and help Mother lay the table," Liz said to David and his parents. "Carol and Patsy have nearly finished now and they'll join us when they've put their harness away." The group moved off. David looked very indignant.

"Liz, that's awfully bad news for Carol. She looked really upset. Can we do anything to help?"

"I don't know," Liz looked thoughtful, "you'll have to give Carol time, you know, just let things take their course. She finds it difficult to admit she's disabled, and has fought so hard to be accepted. It will have been a real blow that she may not be able to

17

go to camp."

"Yes, but we ought to do something," David went on, "couldn't we talk to Ann and Ian, they were super at camp, we could ask them to have Carol over for an assessment or something?"

"I expect our parents will talk to Ann and Ian if we ask them, but you and I could write a letter with Patsy. I don't think we should tell Carol, because if it didn't work she'd feel even worse. We must give it a lot of thought. I'm not sure she'd like the idea of an assessment."

"Aren't you going to Windsor?" David suddenly asked. "Do you remember that Ann said they are going to Windsor to compete? Maybe she and Ian could watch Carol and Patsy in their class, then they would be able to see how competent they are as a team."

"That's a brilliant idea," Liz said admiringly, "because we could set that up without Carol and Patsy even knowing."

Lunch was a fun meal. To her surprise Carol found it easy to get on with David's parents who treated her exactly like the others and didn't seem bothered by her crutches and wheelchair. Patsy was chattering away, sat between David and Liz.

"Carol," she called across the table, "David's had a great idea for this afternoon. He's suggested that we set out a scurry course and I backstep for Liz and he backsteps for you. Then he and Liz can show us what they learnt at camp."

Oh, well, Carol thought, I'm just going to have to join in. She smiled at Patsy. "OK, we'll let the experts teach us!"

18

CHAPTER IV.

It was still rather grey and overcast after lunch when they carried the cones out into the field to make the course, and there were one or two darker clouds that looked a bit ominous.

"I hope we don't get the course set up," puffed Patsy with a cone in each hand, "only to find it tips with rain."

"This is the same as the one we built at camp," Liz said to Carol as they took their cones further up the field, "so we know the distances are about right." Harnessing up didn't take long, but Carol and David had to re-balance Paddy's exercise cart as David obviously weighed a lot more that Patsy.

"Are you taking Paddy to Windsor?" he asked Carol.

"No," Carol explained, "we haven't done much with Paddy. I was only given him at Easter after our holiday in Southern Ireland. Today will be the farthest we've ever driven him, and the first time he's been away from home for more than a short drive. He's pretty fit now, but I mustn't do too much with him, we've a long drive home as well."

"I'd forgotten that," David stepped onto the backstep as Carol moved off towards the field. He called to Liz and Patsy, "you'd better go first, and Carol and I will watch. Carol doesn't want to wear Paddy out, they've got to get home later."

"O.K." Liz drove into the field and started to warm Harmony up.

"I'll just walk Paddy round quietly to keep him moving," Carol said. It was strange with David behind her, she was so used to Patsy. She looked across to the other vehicle and laughed. "I'm used to Patsy's non-stop chatter," she said. "I wonder if Liz will find it distracting!"

"I've got a little sister about her age," David smiled, "she talks all the time too."

"Patsy's not a baby," Carol said, immediately on the defensive, "she's pretty grown up for twelve, and I'm only one year older." David didn't say anything, he was watching Liz and Patsy with Harmony.

"Liz does drive well," he exclaimed, "I thought that at camp with the ponies there, but Harmony's a smashing pony, isn't he?"

"Haven't you seen Liz drive him before?" Carol felt better, he was obviously impressed. "Liz taught me to drive with Harmony, he's super."

"I bet he hasn't scurried before," David called across to the other vehicle, "come on Liz, he must be warmed up by now."

"Right, here we go." Liz picked up a rein in each hand, said something to Patsy, then pushed her bottom back on the seat, braced her feet and leaned forward. She trotted the course quite calmly first, and then came over to Carol and David.

"I think Harmony's wondering what on earth is going on!" she said gaily. "Do you want to have a go now, or shall I try at canter?"

"You have another turn," Carol replied, "I want to watch you cantering." She did watch intently to see where Liz started to turn on the bends.

"Well done!" they both called as Harmony cantered through the finish.

"It wasn't very fast," Liz brought Harmony to stand beside Paddy, "I thought I'd better not race him round yet, he's still getting the hang of it."

"Your turn, Carol," Patsy cried excitedly, "let's see how you get on." A determined look came over Carol's face as she moved off.

"Paddy, trot on!" she called, she had been watching Liz carefully. I think I'll be able to canter once I've got going, she thought to herself. Paddy's smaller than Harmony, so I've got the advantage of more space. "Hang on, David," she said and set off briskly for the first cones. Once through she leaned forward and urged Paddy into canter. "Come on, Paddy," she encouraged the little piebald, "come on." She concentrated hard on aiming for the middle of the cones, she could feel David shifting his weight from side to side and realised he was helping the vehicle round corners. "No cones down this time, Patsy!" she cried triumphantly as she pushed Paddy faster through the finish. She pulled the little pony up. "You are a good boy," she told him.

"He was great," said David enthusiastically, "he was really nippy round the bends."

"You were leaning to help on the bends, weren't you? Carol looked at David, "It made a lot of difference."

"Yes, they taught us that at camp," said David, jumping down and going to Paddy's head, "let's watch Liz and Patsy try for a faster round."

"Didn't he go well?" Patsy's face was full of pride, as she looked at Carol and Paddy, "I thought he was brilliant."

"You and Liz have another go. We'll time you and then try and beat your time." Carol said shifting herself on the driving seat.

"Good idea," David looked at his watch, "tell me when they start." Patsy and Liz headed for the start.

"Now," Carol cried as the pair set off again. "Oh look, David, they've got a cone down."

"That's five seconds to add to their time." David watched as they finished without further fault. "One minute twenty seconds," he called to Liz, "I've added five seconds for your one cone down."

"How mean!" Liz exclaimed. "I'm going to have another try while we're steamed up and raring to go."

"With eight miles to drive, one more turn will be enough for Paddy." Carol said to David as they watched Liz trying to beat her previous time. This time Harmony flew round and Carol noticed that Patsy had got the hang of moving on the backstep to help swing the vehicle round the corners.

"One minute eight seconds," called David as they cantered clear through the finish. "We'll have a job to beat that. You'd better have my watch, Liz, so we use the same timer for both of us." He unstrapped his watch and handed it to Liz as Harmony came back to them, "you've given us a real challenge, haven't they Carol?"

"Well, we've nothing to lose," Carol was determined to make it a good fight. "Come on David, we'll give them a run for their money!" Paddy seemed to have woken up this time as they headed for the start, and, for him, set off at quite a cracking pace. Carol was taken unawares, and was late shortening her reins. She hadn't really got into position for the first cones and turning for the next set, lurched sideways. David, on the backstep, grabbed her anorak.

"Brace your feet, Carol!" he cried. Carol managed to push back against the seat and more by luck than judgment slid into a better position for the next pair of cones. "Slow him a bit," David said

21

quietly. He suddenly realised that Carol simply didn't have the strength in her legs. He leaned forward and hanging on with one hand kept a tight hold of Carol's anorak with the other. Paddy slowed slightly and Carol hung on grimly to retain her balance as they turned through the rest of the cones and headed out through the finish. It all happened so quickly. Once through the little piebald slowed up of his own accord. David quietly let go of Carol's anorak as Patsy cried excitedly.

"We've won, we've won, you were one minute twelve seconds!"

"Take him round the field at walk to cool off," David suggested to Carol. He could sense she was upset. He wondered if it was because she'd been beaten, or because she'd nearly fallen out. He didn't know if the other two had noticed. "Well done the winners!" he called gaily as Carol turned the exercise cart and walked up the field. "We'll just cool Paddy down before you get the chance to crow over your victory!" By the time they'd got back to Patsy and Liz , Paddy was hardly puffing. David jumped down and went to Paddy's head. Carol didn't look at him.

"You were too fast for us," she said to Liz and Patsy. "We shall have to call it a day with the long drive ahead. I think I'd better take Paddy back and let him have a rest." Then she looked round at David. "Thank you, David, I couldn't have managed without you." Her eyes, large in her rather pale face, pleaded with him not to say anything. Not yet, I feel all bounced about and need time, she thought. David did a mock bow.

"Your servant, Madam! I'll hand you back to Patsy now, and go back to the stables with Liz."

"O.K. I'll take over." Patsy came across and jumped up behind. "I've learnt a lot," she said happily to Carol. "It's great fun isn't it?"

"Yes," Carol turned to look at her friend, "but I'm not going to be able to go much faster than we did today."

"Paddy will pep up," Patsy replied, "he got going well the last time, although Liz and I thought you looked a bit unbalanced through the first cones."

"I don't mean Paddy won't be able to do it." Carol looked at Patsy, "didn't you see? If David hadn't been so quick and grabbed my anorak, I'd have been bounced out."

"Oh, fiddle, your legs!" Patsy had spent so much time with Carol, she was quick to understand. "Couldn't you brace yourself enough?"

"No, and I got dreadfully shaken around. David held onto me all the way and I managed to slow Paddy up. If he hadn't been such a good pony and David so quick to realise what was happening, I could have had a nasty accident."

"David didn't say anything," Patsy said slowly, "that was good of him."

"I think he realised I needed a bit of time to recover," Carol said, "he positively ordered me to walk Paddy away from you two to cool off. I needed time to cool off too! I was so disappointed. I'm not going to be able to scurry in competitions, Patsy, I just couldn't do the speed, my legs couldn't cope with the strain. It's no good pretending. I shall have to do it all more slowly, for fun."

"Well, there are lots of other things you can do, and your parents will probably be jolly relieved." Patsy said sensibly. They reached the stable yard. Liz and David were already unharnessing Harmony.

"Come on, you slow coaches," Liz called, "I'm dying for my tea. It's thirsty work cone driving, despite the grey sky."

Carol found by the time they'd dealt with Paddy and turned him out for a rest she was glad to get into her wheelchair. Her legs were beginning to ache. She thought rather dismally of the long drive home. Usually it was such fun, but another good two hours driving could be a bit much. Perhaps a break would help.

After tea they sat around sprawled on the chairs in the Roberts lounge, the adults were washing up in the kitchen. David spoke in a very matter of fact way.

"You know, Carol, I've had an idea. It's so much harder for you with legs not as strong as most people, and I wondered if a marathon strap would help? I think it's amazing what you can do but turning round those cones at speed must be difficult. My father competes at horse driving trials, and for the marathon phase most of the whips wear a big wide belt to keep them in place. You simply couldn't risk the driver leaving his seat if the vehicle lurched through an obstacle, he has to stay on board and keep control of his horses."

"I don't think I'll ever be able to scurry properly," Carol

looked bravely at David, then turned to Liz, "David hasn't told you, but if he hadn't grabbed my anorak I think I'd have been bounced out the last time we went round the cones." She paused, "you were great, David, thanks. I think a strap might be well worth a try. Could you ask your father for me, but not until you get home? I don't want Mummy and Daddy to hear what happened, and forbid me to have another go."

"That's O.K., and I'll tell you what, Carol," David went on, "Paddy was really good, he didn't take advantage at all when you lost your balance. Most ponies would have dashed off, but he slowed down as soon as you recovered and told him to, didn't he?" Carol nodded, then she looked out of the window.

"Oh, help! Look it's raining." As she spoke Mrs. Roberts came in from the kitchen.

"Carol, it's beginning to rain quite steadily. I don't think you can drive home in this, would you like us to run you and Patsy home, and then your mother can pop you over tomorrow after school to drive Paddy back?" She looked questioningly at Carol. "Liz goes back to school this evening, so I'm going to have to break the party up, and you and Carol start again tomorrow, don't you?"

"Yes, we do." Carol smiled, "That's very kind of you, but I expect Mummy would come and fetch us now if I 'phoned her, because you'll want to leave with Liz, won't you?"

"Maybe that would be best," Mrs. Roberts turned to Liz, "I'm sorry to be boring, darling, but you ought to get yourself ready soon." The Templars came in from the kitchen to join them all.

"It's been a lovely day, and nice to meet you again, but we must go." David got up, and moved to the door.

"I'll collect up my things," he turned to the girls, "bye Carol, bye Patsy, I'll see you soon, no doubt, possibly at Windsor if I can persuade mother and father to go." He went out with Liz. Carol got up to go and phone her mother.

By the time Mrs. Lane had driven over the Templars and David had already left, and Liz was ready to leave for school. "See you at Windsor!" She called, as she waved them good-bye. "I've got an exeat that weekend, thank goodness, so we'll be there."

CHAPTER V

The week before the Windsor Show flew by. Patsy and Carol found their days were very full. Patsy cycled over to Old Chimneys in the mornings . Mrs. Lane took both girls into school, and collected them afterwards. They had tea in the kitchen or on the lawn if it was nice, and then they started work with the ponies. They groomed each pony in turn, working together. Neither Paddy nor Pinto minded Carol's wheelchair any more and she could wheel herself alongside to groom what she described as 'the middle bit.' Patsy picked out the feet and Carol started her section while Patsy went the other side to do the top line.

"It's a good job the ponies are only 12.2hh," she remarked one evening as they brushed away busily. "If we had anything larger I'd only be able to reach a small piece to clean."

"It's a good job they're both so quiet and well behaved," Patsy replied, "just imagine if they fidgeted, or swung round, or kicked!" She ran a hand over the glossy coat, "you're a good boy, Pinto," she crooned happily. Paddy stood a little further away, tied to a ring on the stable wall. He'd already been groomed, and for a short while his unruly mane had been tamed; combed and damped down it looked neat and tidy for a change. Carol looked across at him with satisfaction.

"Paddy looks very different now," she commented to Patsy as she knocked her curry comb clean against the side of her wheelchair. "We've got him looking as smart as Pinto. I wish we were taking him to Windsor too. He'll feel so lonely on his own while we're away."

"Perhaps next year we'll be able to take both if you've learnt to drive them as a pair," Patsy said hopefully.

"I've got to learn somehow," Carol stopped and put the body brush in her lap, "after Windsor I shall have to work on Mummy and Daddy to let me have lessons." Patsy fetched the harness and while she was putting it on Carol's mother appeared with a lunge line in her hand.

"If you take the exercise cart and drive out down the road to the village and back up the lane, I'll lunge Paddy for half an hour. When you get back we'll make a list for Windsor."

"Only two days to go," Patsy said as she pulled the exercise cart up to Pinto and began fastening the traces. "It's getting exciting, I always enjoy the days before a show, with all the planning and anticipation." Mrs. Lane smiled. She put the lunge line down and came to give the girls a hand.

"Ready?" she asked Carol, who climbed into the cart, and her mother strapped her crutches on the back. Patsy moved round and as Carol set off she hopped onto the backstep and waved good-bye to Mrs. Lane.

The evening was sunny and mild, with the hedges heavy with leaves and blossom which filled the air with summer scents. Pinto trotted briskly, his muscles rippling under his shining coat. They reached the village and turned along the rather narrow lane which led back behind the vicarage to Old Chimneys.

"Do you remember when we tipped Reuban's cart into the ditch?" Patsy laughed as they passed the gateway where Carol had tried to turn to get away from a lorry when they had first discovered Pinto was a driving pony.

"It seems a long time ago," Carol slowed Pinto back to a walk. "We were real beginners, and Mummy and Daddy weren't a bit keen for me to drive, were they?"

"No, they nearly stopped us then, but now they're as keen as they were when you used to show ponies." Carol let Pinto walk the last half mile home. "We've done a lot since then," Patsy went on, "I just hope we do well at Windsor this year after all the work everyone has put in." They turned up the drive. Paddy was rolling out in the paddock, his mane had fallen back into its normal untidy state. It wasn't long before Patsy led Pinto through the paddock gate to join him.

Carol and Patsy were very busy during the next few days. What they were completely unaware of was the plotting and planning being carried out by two other sets of people, their parents and Liz and David. Mrs. Lane and Mrs. Leigh had written a letter to the Magpie Carriage Driving Centre to see if they could persuade Ian and Ann, the owners, to accept Carol with Patsy, for the able bodied junior camp. The Reverend Leigh had written a separate letter extolling Carol's courage in battling against her disabilities. Mr. and Mrs. Roberts had contributed a third letter, Mrs. Roberts explaining that she had taught Carol from the beginning, and that

26

Carol had reached a very good standard for a girl of her age.

Liz and David put together a personal plea asking that Ann and Ian went to watch Carol at Windsor where she and Patsy were entered in the Junior Novice Whip class. They could say that, as they had been at a camp, they knew Carol and Patsy would be of a high enough standard, and that Patsy had always groomed for Carol, so they wouldn't need any extra help.

As the letters kept arriving at the Magpie Carriage Driving Centre Ian and Ann began to feel they must perhaps reconsider. "I don't know about you Ian," Ann remarked as she opened Liz and David's letter four days before the Windsor Show. "Here's another letter about Carol Lane. I'm beginning to feel hounded! I think we shall have to go and watch the child drive. The trouble is, if we accept one disabled child to the junior whip camp we may find others who feel they should be there too. Some of our disabled whips have a high standard of driving."

"It's no good worrying about that yet," Ian remarked, taking the letter from Ann so he could read it as well. "Liz and David drove to a pretty good standard, second best of their week, and actually I'm not sure they shouldn't have won. It was a very close decision. They would know better than anyone whether this girl could cope with camp. As the children sleep out in the two barns, there isn't a problem with stairs anywhere, and we have a downstairs toilet. I suggest we watch the class at Windsor and then maybe if we think she is a possibility we could ask her over to see whether we shall need any special facilities."

Windsor was wet. The arriving horse boxes and trailers had to drive over special metalled tracks to reach the parking area. It had started to rain the day before and Carol and Patsy had nearly driven Mr. and Mrs. Lane mad. "When do you think it will stop raining?" Patsy asked dismally for about the sixth time, trailing into the kitchen behind Mrs. Lane, leaving wet footprints and drips off her coat all over the floor.

"Patsy, leave your boots on the mat!" Mrs. Lane was cross, "and I can't tell you when it will stop raining. I only know the weather forecast is not good. Go and tell Carol that Pinto must be left in the stable tonight to make sure he's clean and dry ready for an early start."

It was still raining the next morning when they woke. Packing the horsebox in the rain was horrid, only Pinto seemed his usual happy self.

"I am glad we sold the trailer and bought this horsebox." Mr. Lane looked across the showground as they arrived to try and spot a good parking place. "It's a bit bigger than we need at present, but at least there is room for both ponies if we ever need to take two, and the phaeton."

"Yes," Mrs. Lane agreed, "we could just squeeze the exercise cart and Pinto into the old trailer, but the lorry gives us much more space and more options."

"You girls can go and get your number," Mr.Lane said as he pulled the horsebox up and turned off the engine. He got out and went round to get Carol's wheelchair out. "Oh dear," he said, "It is very wet underfoot, I'm not sure you're going to be able to use your chair much. Patsy had better go on her own."

"I'll get the coffee ready." Mrs. Lane said quickly, looking at Carol's gloomy face. "Don't worry, it will probably clear up later."

"It's beastly!" Carol exclaimed despondently. "I'm not going to be much help if the showground gets muddy. Not with a wheelchair and crutches, it will be almost impossible to get about."

"As long as we can get you to the ring clean, that's the most important thing," her mother handed her a cup of coffee from the flask. "Patsy will be back in a minute and then we can start getting ourselves organised."

"I wonder if Liz and her family have arrived yet?" Carol held her steaming mug of coffee and peered out into the rain. "You and Daddy thought you'd been so extravagant, buying a horsebox with a living area, but it's going to be wonderful today. We can all sit in comfort, and it won't be nearly as cramped as in the car." Patsy and Mr. Lane came back together. Mr. Lane had gone to see where the ring was, and had met Patsy as she returned from the secretary's tent. They climbed into the living area of the box, shaking the worst of the rain off first.

"I think it's eased a little," Mr. Lane put his wet coat down away from the seats. "I suppose it's the same for everyone, but it's really most unpleasant."

Carol was quite surprised that they didn't see the Roberts at all.

28

Liz wasn't eligible for the Novice Junior Whip Class as she had won classes before, so she was entering the Open Class for Juniors which was later in the day. By the time Carol and Patsy were dressed and ready it had at last stopped raining, but Carol found it very frustrating because she couldn't help at all in case she got wet and muddy. Her crutches would have stuck in the mud and the wheelchair would be even worse. It was her parents who got Pinto ready and put to. They lifted Carol and Patsy onto the phaeton, and followed them to the collecting ring, carrying a bucket of water and a cloth.

"Last year we did everything ourselves." Carol said sadly as she drove Pinto across the showground.

"Well, we're jolly lucky to have your parents as a back up team," Patsy said, "look at the mud splashing onto our beautiful paintwork, it took us hours to clean and shine it up. Your parents are brilliant, following with a bucket and cloth to clean off the splashes before we go into the ring. We'd better do them justice today."

"You're right, of course," Carol replied, neatly manoeuvering Pinto around a mother trying to get along with her child in a pushchair. "Look, that's what it would be like for me in a wheelchair today, but I just feel so pathetic not being able to do things as I usually can."

"It is pretty exceptional to have quite such wet weather," Patsy remarked, "you'll just have to put up with it." They reached the collecting ring and checked in with the ring steward. Mr. and Mrs. Lane started to wash off the worst of the mud.

"Oh, look!" Carol suddenly saw Liz and David in the distance. "Who are they talking to?"

"I don't know, I can't really see, but the woman looks familiar. Oh, Liz has seen us, she's waving."

"Is she coming over?" Carol asked, "I don't think she is. How strange, she always comes to wish us luck."

"The ring steward's beckoning us, Carol." Patsy interrupted. "He wants us in the ring."

"Good luck." Mr. and Mrs. Lane called, as Carol collected Pinto up and went towards the ring entrance. Once inside the ring Carol forgot about the onlookers at the ropes. She loved the feeling of performing for the judge and Pinto always responded

29

too. he was such a perky, happy pony. He almost shouted out 'look at me, I'm having fun.' He hadn't the elegance of some of the showier ponies, but he had character and presence, and always looked as if he was enjoying what he was doing. Carol and Patsy hadn't driven the phaeton in a show ring before, and they felt rather grand. It was a lovely vehicle, which Charles Godber had bid for on their behalf at the Reading Carriage Sales over a year ago.

Mr. and Mrs. Lane stood by the ring ropes and watched with pride. "I'm glad Carol persuaded us to let her drive," Mrs. Lane said contentedly, "they really do look good, don't they?"

"I think we might be a little biased," Mr. Lane laughed at his wife, "but I must say I think they look the best in the ring."

"But will the judges?" Mrs. Lane queried. "I'm still not sure we really understand what the judge is looking for where driving ability is concerned. I do know that Pinto is very fit and looks good, and the vehicle, the harness, and the girls are as immaculate as anyone could be in these conditions."

"I think they like Carol today," Mr. Lane was jubilant, "look, they've been pulled in second in the line up." Patsy hopped out and went and stood in front of Pinto while the judge walked down the line looking carefully at each turnout. He checked the harness, looked all round each vehicle, and made comments to his steward who was making notes. When he had inspected the whole line his steward indicated to the first vehicle that they could start their display. Carol watched carefully, and as the turnout came back Patsy hopped up beside Carol and they moved out into the ring.

Somehow Patsy knew everything was going well. She just felt Carol was completely confident and Pinto was responding like a dream. He lengthened his stride and produced a lovely extended trot, and then came back to collection the minute Carol asked him. As they moved back into position she whispered to Carol, "That was great, Carol, better than the first lot." Carol relaxed slightly and glanced sideways at Patsy.

"It felt good, Pinto was super, he did his very best." They had quite a long wait while all the vehicles gave an individual show, before the steward sent them out to walk round the ring while the judge made his final decision.

Patsy sat bolt upright, looking straight ahead, her gloved hands in her lap. She was praying the judge would have liked them best. They'd never won a first rosette, and to win at Windsor would be very special. She heard Carol give a gasp, and then turn the phaeton into the centre. "Wow!" she said very quietly under her breath to Carol, still looking straight ahead. "I think we've done it." When the judge came up to give Carol her rosette, he also handed her a silver cup.

"Congratulations, my dear. I haven't seen you in the show ring before, and you drove very well. How long have you been driving?"

"Nearly two years," Carol replied, "but last year we weren't ready for this class, so we did the road safety competition instead." The judge smiled, "You've got a very nice turnout and a lovely little pony. You should be proud of him," and he turned to move on.

"Thank you." Carol was so delighted she almost forgot, "Thank you so much," she called again, and the judge turned and touched his bowler hat.

"My pleasure," he said.

Carol handed the cup to Patsy. "You'd better hold this," she said, "and for heavens sake be careful the base doesn't fall off, or the lid, or something."

"It's very smart, isn't it?" Patsy held it rather gingerly. They felt very proud driving a circuit of the ring in the lead, and Carol looked round excitedly as they drove back into the collecting ring. Her parents were waiting with big smiles on their faces.

"Well done, darling!" Mrs. Lane cried.

31

As they made their way back to the box Carol looked at Patsy. "I still can't understand why Liz and David haven't been to see us," she said. "Liz always comes, she is one of our team, and she will be so pleased for us. It's very strange." Patsy nodded in agreement, she couldn't understand it either.

While they unharnessed Pinto and put him back into the horsebox they made a great fuss of the little piebald pony. They'd just given him a big haynet to pull at, and Patsy was helping Carol back to the living area when Liz's voice rang out from behind them. "Well done, you two. Well driven Carol, you looked super." Carol and Patsy turned. Liz and David were stood there and behind them the two people they had been with earlier. Both Carol and Patsy recognized them now they were closer.

"Oh. Hallo," Carol said rather uncertainly.

Liz went on, "Do you remember Ann and Ian?" She was bubbling with excitement. "David suggested that we asked them to come and watch you drive at Windsor, but we didn't expect you to put on a winning performance for them. They've got something to say to you Carol."

"The first thing is congratulations to you both," Ian stepped forward and smiled at Carol, "You've got quite a fan club you know." Carol looked puzzled. "We've had a flood of letters," he went on, "saying you would cope easily with our junior whip camp, and, after watching you today, Ann and I feel if you and Patsy would like to come, you'd be very welcome." Carol stared at them.

"Really?" she asked, "really, even though I'm disabled?"

Ann put her hand onto Carol's arm. "Yes," she said, "you drive very well and your groom is excellent." She grinned at Patsy. "I understand the two of you are quite a team." Patsy beamed with pleasure.

"Please come and tell Carol's parents," she said, "they'll be so thrilled." Ann and Ian followed with Liz and David as Patsy helped Carol with her crutches through the mud and into the box. It was quite a squash, everybody was talking at once and Patsy proudly stood the cup, with the rosette tied on one of the handles, on the shelf by the kettle. Mrs. Lane got out a box of biscuits and made tea. Suddenly Carol looked at Liz. "Isn't it nearly time for your class?"

Liz looked rather sad. "I'm not competing," she said slowly, "we didn't tell you because we didn't want to worry you before your class. We had to get the vet. out to Harmony last night, he had an attack of colic, and we still don't know what caused it. David's parents brought us today. Harmony's much better this morning but Mummy didn't want to leave him."

"How awful!" Carol and Patsy both looked very upset. "He will be all right, won't he?" Carol asked. Liz nodded. Carol turned to Ian and Ann. "I learnt to drive with Liz and Harmony. Harmony is very special." Suddenly her face lit up. "I know, Liz," she cried, "you can take Pinto and the phaeton, and Patsy will groom for you, won't you Patsy?"

Patsy nodded. "What a good idea."

"You're really kind," Liz replied, "I'd love to, but I've told the secretary I won't be competing." Mr. Lane interrupted.

"I'll go and see the secretary straight away," he cried, getting up. "I'm sure she'd understand."

"But I haven't brought my clothes," Liz sounded flustered

"Wear mine!" said Carol, "I know you're taller than me, but you're ever so slim and if the skirt is very short no one will know under a driving apron."

It was a mad rush to get ready. David went to help Mrs. Lane, Ian and Ann get Pinto out of the horsebox, and clean up the phaeton once again. Carol stripped off her navy blue skirt, jacket and blouse and put on her jeans and a sweater. Liz tried on the blouse.

"It's a bit tight across the bust," she said, "I hope the buttons don't burst off!" Patsy giggled.

"I shall laugh if they do. I shouldn't be able to keep a straight face if we're driving round the ring and I hear one pop off!"

"Do you mind? Pinto is your pony." Liz turned to Patsy, "I think I can get away with Carol's clothes, though they are a bit tight, but the hat looks all right, doesn't it?"

"I think it's great," Patsy was full of enthusiasm. "I'm getting the hang of being a groom. It's fun, and I did groom for you at the Forest Show two years ago." She brushed some mud off her

33

jodhpurs. "I'm not quite as clean as I was, I wasn't expecting to perform again."

Mrs. Lane appeared at the door. "Are you ready?" she asked. "The secretary is happy for you to compete with a replacement turnout, but you ought to be going to the ring."

"Take me with you and Patsy," Carol said as they helped her out of the box, "otherwise I'll never make the ring in time. If Mummy gives me my crutches I can lean on them at the ringside, and then you can give me a lift back again afterwards."

It was all a bit of a scramble but they managed to get to the collecting ring with a few minutes to spare. Mr Lane helped Carol down and they made slow progress to the ring edge. Ian and Ann following looked at each other. "They're a nice bunch of kids," Ian said, "look how Carol struggles on those crutches in this mud. Yet when she was in the ring you would never have known she was disabled."

"She never hesitated either." Ann went on, " she offered Liz her turnout without even thinking about it. That was very generous."

The little group stood watching from the ring side. "Has Liz driven Pinto before?" Ann asked. "She seems to be doing well."

"Oh, yes," Patsy turned towards Ann, "she's driven Pinto lots, but with the exercise cart. We're only allowed the phaeton for show practice, so Liz never has the opportunity to drive it."

"Liz is very experienced," Carol added, " she's driven in so many shows. Before she learnt to drive, and before I had my accident, we used to ride in show pony classes. We started off in lead rein classes competing against each other, and then Liz's parents bought Harmony for the first ridden classes. When she outgrew him, they started driving him, that must have been at least four years ago."

"This class is of a very high standard," Ian was studying all the other turnouts, "and some of the children look quite old, but then sixteen year olds are sophisticated today."

David leaned on the rail willing Liz to do well. He didn't think he would want to compete in the show ring, they all looked very professional, and he knew it took a lot of spit and polish to reach this standard. He thought he would rather follow in his father's footsteps and have a go at horse driving trials, at least there you

34

only had to be smart for presentation and dressage. His musing was interrupted by Carol, who put her hand on his arm.

"David," she said rather shyly, "do you think if I lean on the rail, you could pull my crutch out of the mud. This right one has sunk in and stuck." David turned and smiled at her.

"Here," he said, "hang on to me, I wouldn't trust that rail. Then I'll pull your crutch out. It really is awfully muddy underfoot, isn't it?" he pulled the crutch out of the muddy patch. "I should move this way a bit." He showed her a small piece of ground less trampled and squelchy, and helped Carol move onto it. "How's Liz doing, do you think?" he asked anxiously.

"Brilliantly." Carol replied, looking back into the ring. " Look, she's gone into fourth place in the preliminary line up."

"But I thought she often won in these classes?" David queried.

"Yes, she does, but to drive a strange vehicle, cold with no warm up, straight into a ring in a class of this standard in someone else's clothes, is not easy. I think she's doing incredibly well, you've just heard Ian saying the standard is very high."

By the time Liz and Pinto had to do their individual show, Liz had adjusted to the different vehicle and to the onlooker's delight ended up placed second.

It was quite a day, Carol thought as she finally snuggled down under her duvet hours later. It had started off rather badly with the rain and the wet conditions, but once the rain had actually stopped the weather hadn't mattered except for that awful mud. Pinto had been the star. Their very first driving cup together was special, he had gone so well, and then for Liz to come second with him in the Open Junior Whip Class was amazing. It was a top quality class at one of the biggest shows of the year, so it was a huge feather in his cap. Now on top of those two wonderful achievements she had the summer junior whip camp to look forward to as well. She yawned sleepily, driving a pair might be a possibility after all.

Ironically the next day when Carol awoke the sun was shining through her bedroom window. As soon as she was dressed Carol made her way to the telephone in the hall and dialed the Roberts number. "How's Harmony Liz?" she asked anxiously as soon as she heard Liz answer at the other end.

"He's fine," Liz sounded very cheerful, "we still don't know what caused the colic, but it wasn't a very bad attack because the vet. was able to deal with it promptly. He's taken a couple of dung samples away for worm analysis, but as we worm the horses every six weeks he doesn't think that is the cause. I don't expect we'll ever know." She paused, and then went on "By the way Mummy sends congratulations on winning your class, she was really pleased."

"Thanks, I still can't quite believe it." Carol was still on cloud nine.

"What about the weather?" Liz went on, "can you believe the lovely sunshine today? It's so unfair after all that rain and mud yesterday."

"I know, just our bad luck, I suppose." Carol shifted her crutches and leaned more comfortably against the wall. "I wanted to thank you and David, and everyone else for writing to Ann and Ian about the summer camp. I'm so thrilled that Patsy and I can go. It will be such fun, and I wanted to ask you about the exams you took. I've decided I'd like to have a go at them as well. I have more time sitting about than most people so I could do some of the theory work in advance, couldn't I? I'd like to do well."

"O.K. I'll bring the syllabus with me the next time I see you. It was great of you, Carol, to lend me your clothes, Pinto and the phaeton. Pinto was wonderful, wasn't he?" The two girls chatted on for some time, finally Mrs. Lane interrupted them when she came out of the kitchen.

"Carol," she exclaimed, "I didn't realise you were up. I was just coming to wake you. I'll go and put your breakfast on. Now don't be long on that 'phone."

When Carol joined her mother in the kitchen there was a delicious smell of grilling bacon and she sniffed in appreciation. "I'm awfully hungry," she said, "I'm sorry I overslept, Mummy, I expect you've been out to do Paddy and Pinto by now." Her mother deftly slid a fried egg out of the pan onto a plate and added two rashers of bacon from the grill.

"Yes, I did them early, and I've turned them out." she replied, handing the plate to Carol. "I thought you'd be tired after yesterday. How are the legs?" Carol grimaced.

"A bit stiff and weary," she admitted, "but I'm sure the stiffness will wear off fairly quickly." As Carol ate her breakfast they discussed the happenings of the day before, and Carol told her mother of her plan to start work before the summer camp, so that she would be better prepared to take her B.D.S. level one exam.

"I think that's a splendid idea, Carol," her mother was enthusiastic, "as long as you don't let your end of term work suffer."

CHAPTER VII

"What's that lorry doing parked across the end of our drive?" Mrs. Lane came round the corner of the house a few weekends later. They both stopped and stared. It was a rather elderly battered lorry with what looked like a load of scrap metal on the back. As they watched a man jumped down from the lorry cab and peered over the hedge into the paddock where Paddy and Pinto were peacefully grazing. Carol looked frightened. "It couldn't be horse thieves, could it, Mummy?" she asked anxiously. "There have been horses stolen from paddocks recently. Perhaps we ought to ring the police."

"Thank goodness we've had them freeze branded." Mrs. Lane said. "I think that is a big deterrent. Thieves know that the number freeze branded onto the animal can be checked, and the horses should not be sold without the correct papers."

"Look!" Carol exclaimed, "he's seen us watching." The man hesitated, and turned towards his lorry. Then he obviously changed his mind because he turned round and started to walk up the drive towards them.

"Who on earth can that be?" Mrs. Lane exclaimed, but Carol had seen a familiar red scarf knotted round the man's neck.

"It's Reuban!" She cried excitedly, and started down the drive on her crutches. Mrs. Lane followed more slowly. She had never felt completely easy with the gypsies, but the three girls were quite at home with them.

"Reuban," Carol called , "what are you doing?" She moved as fast as her crutches would let her.

Reuban Smith stopped in front of her, his dark, tanned face had a welcoming smile.

"Hallo, missy," he pointed towards the paddock. "I were just passing and I thought me eyes were playing tricks. I had to stop and have a proper look. You've got another Pinto then?" Carol laughed.

"He's called Paddy, and I was given him as a present from someone in Ireland. He's very quiet to drive." Then suddenly she thought back to the Windsor weekend. "Oh, Reuban," she said, "you will be proud of Pinto. We took him to the Royal Windsor

Horse Show, and he won a silver cup with me in the novice junior whip class, and then was second with Liz driving in the open class."

"He never did!" Reuban exclaimed. "What a clever little 'hoss. It was a good day when you started driving him." He looked uneasily across to Mrs. Lane who had walked to join them. "Good afternoon to you, Maam" he said touching his rather dirty old cap. "Begging your pardon for mentioning it, but when I was looking at them ponies I see'd there's a weak place in your hedge just there by the corner." He pointed over to the far corner of the paddock where it joined the road.

"Thank you," Mrs. Lane said stiffly, "I'll get my husband to see to it."

"You don't want them little ponies getting on the road." Reuban looked back at Carol. "Do the other little pony really drive?" he asked. Carol nodded.

"Yes, I'm hoping one day to learn to drive them as a pair. They are nearly a perfect match." Reuban turned to go.

"Good luck to you both," he touched his cap again, "I hope you get your wish, they'd be smart as a pair." He walked back down the drive. Carol called after him.

"Are you staying in the vicarage orchard?"

"Not this time, missy." He half turned. "I'm going through to the Cotswolds to sell a pony, and I called this way to collect some scrap from the farm up the road."

"Patsy will be sorry she hasn't seen the gypsies." Carol watched him stride away to the lorry, get into the cab and drive off. "They nearly always stay at the vicarage." Mrs. Lane looked rather relieved.

"Well, it was good of him to tell us about the hedge," she remarked, trying to be fair, "let's go and have a look." There was a thin patch by the corner. The ponies had obviously been standing there pushing against the hedge, but the two strands of wire were quite taut. "I don't think they can get out, but I'll tell your father and maybe he can strengthen it tomorrow." They made their way slowly back to the house.

Patsy cycled over at tea time.

"I wish I'd seen Reuban, I think he's great," she said wistfully as she took a mug of tea from Mrs. Lane and put it down on the

39

grass. They were having tea in their favourite spot in the shade of the beech tree by the side of the lawn. Mrs. Lane turned the conversation back to safer channels. She had never thought the Smiths were very desirable friends for the girls, but she knew they owed them a lot. Reuban Smith had given Pinto to the vicar for his children some years ago, and later had helped Carol when she was fighting to prove she could drive well enough to compete in the show ring.

"The BDS Show at Smith's Lawn in a couple of weeks time is our next show. We've entered Pinto, but Daddy and I wondered if you'd like to take Paddy, just to see how he behaves."

"Oh, yes, that would be fun!" Carol said happily, "I'm sure he'd love to come. Could we enter him in anything?"

"We thought he could be entered in the pleasure class for exercise carts, as his first outing."

"That would be just right," Patsy reached for a biscuit. "It would be rather like the first time we took Pinto to a show, and entered the road safety competition because we hadn't used the phaeton enough."

"It's not long to the end of term," Carol remarked. "I can't believe it's June already. After the BDS Show we've got the summer camp to look forward to once the holidays begin."

The next morning when Carol went to the paddock the ponies had gone. At first she thought her mother must have stabled them, but on making her way slowly to the stables she found they were empty too. In a panic she tried to hurry back to the house, cursing her inability to run. When she reached the door she shouted frantically as it opened. The dogs came dashing out ahead of her startled mother.

"Carol! Whatever's the matter?" At almost the same time her father appeared running lightly down the stairs.

"They've gone!" Carol cried, tears starting up in her eyes, "the ponies have gone."

"Nonsense, darling, you just didn't see them," her mother said reassuringly.

"No, they've gone. They're not in the paddock or the stables. I thought you might have put them in. I thought it would take too long for me to check the hedge, so I came straight back. Why didn't we strengthen it after Reuban told us yesterday?"

"I'll go and check." Mr. Lane said curtly, stepping past Carol and running with long strides across to the paddock. He opened the gate and went in. Carol turned on her crutches and she and her mother made their way across slowly. By the time they got there Mr. Lane was back at the gate.

"They went out through the corner," he said grimly.

"But the wire looked fine when we checked it!" Mrs. Lane exclaimed, "I can't believe they broke it."

"They didn't," Mr. Lane looked very stern. "The wire has been cut. I'm afraid they've been stolen!" Carol turned to her mother, despair written all over her face, and burst into tears.

"Not Pinto and Paddy!" she sobbed, "I can't bear it." Her mother put her arms around her.

"I'll go and 'phone the police straight away," said Mr. Lane, "come on Carol, you mustn't get so upset. We must pull ourselves together and work to get them back." he ran back to the house.

"He's right, they can't have been gone long. We must plan the best way to search for them," her mother gave Carol a reassuring squeeze, "we'll get them back."

"Patsy!" Carol exclaimed turning a tear stained face towards her mother. "Pinto belongs to Patsy, we must let the Leighs know. She'll be heartbroken too."

The police came promptly, within half an hour, and Mrs. Leigh and Patsy had already arrived. The policeman sat them all down and asked each one in turn what had happened.

"So you knew the hedge was weak in the corner?" he asked Mrs. Lane.

"Yes, Reuban Smith, the gypsy, told us yesterday. We saw him looking at the ponies over the fence." The policeman looked severe.

"Gypsies!" he said, "we'd better trace them."

"No!" Carol and Patsy cried in unison. "No, Reuban's a Romany, and he wouldn't take our ponies." Patsy went on. "He's our friend, and he gave me Pinto in the first place." Mrs. Leigh spoke quietly.

"My husband is the vicar," she told the policeman, "he has absolute trust in the Smith family. I am sure they wouldn't steal, and certainly not from the girls." The policeman looked sceptical.

" Well, they might be an exception, but it would be unusual."

41

Mrs. Lane explained very clearly what had happened the afternoon before and the policeman noted everything down.

"We shall have to interview this Mr. Smith," he said. Patsy cast an anguished look at Carol. They both knew the Smiths hated involvement with the police, and might blame them for this visit.

When the policeman had gone Mr. Lane outlined his proposed plan of action.

"We must get maximum publicity," he stated, "and that means getting public sympathy. I know you don't like highlighting your disability, Carol, but that is going to be the best way to get support." Carol looked horrified.

"Must we?" she pleaded, "I shall hate it." Patsy looked sadly at her friend.

"It does make sense, Carol," she said.

"Right," Mr. Lane continued, "I will contact the local and national newspapers, local radio and television."

"What can we do?" Mrs. Leigh asked, "and I'm sure that the Roberts will help."

"Your family can contact all the sales and markets, then we'll ask the Roberts to list and 'phone all the abattoirs."

"Thank goodness we had them freeze branded," Mrs. Lane remarked, "I was only saying to Carol yesterday how important that was. They can't be accepted at an abattoir without their papers."

Patsy felt a little better. There was quite a lot could be done.

"Can we offer a reward?" Carol said, "Oh, and surely we must let the freeze brand people know."

"Well thought of," her father agreed, "that is one of the very first things we must do."

Mrs. Lane remarked, "I was only saying to Carol yesterday how important it was. I had no idea we would need to rely on the freeze brands today."

Both Patsy and Carol agreed the rest of the day was a nightmare. As children there really wasn't very much they could do. Their parents were extremely busy telephoning, talking and contacting as many people as possible. One local paper sent a reporter and a photographer out. Carol and Patsy hated every moment of the interview. They were both in tears most of the time. Carol was upset that she seemed to be the object of all the attention.

"Patsy owns Pinto," she pulled Patsy forward, "she's just as upset as I am. She has let me use Pinto and we've been a team together." The photographer took one quick photograph of the two girls together, and then turned back to Carol.

"Let's have another shot of you struggling with your crutches. You need your ponies back, and this will catch public sympathy." Carol posed yet again. "Great," the photographer said happily, "I think that will be the one." He packed his camera away, and he and the reporter left.

CHAPTER VIII

"DISABLED GIRL'S DRIVING PONIES STOLEN." The headline jumped out at Carol from the front page of the Mossminster Daily Echo. She had spent a miserable night half dreaming, half awake imagining all the worst possibilities for Pinto and Paddy. At four o'clock she put her bedside light on to read, hoping to stop her mind churning over and over. A few minutes later there was a tap on the door and her mother came in.

"Daddy and I can't sleep either, darling," she said, "we're going to have a cup of tea in the kitchen. would you like one?" The tea and a change of scene helped. Carol slept afterwards, but she had woken late feeling bleary eyed and very tired. She sat silently at the breakfast table reading the report in the paper.

"The picture's ghastly," she said, "and the writing is sentimental slush, but I suppose if it makes people feel sorry for me and helps bring the ponies back, it's done its job."

"I'll 'phone school and ask if you can have the day off." Mr. Lane looked sympathetically at the pale, wan face across the table.

"Oh, thank you Daddy, I was dreading facing everyone today. They'll all have seen the paper and want to talk about it, and if people are nice to me I shall cry. Perhaps by tomorrow I'll be able to cope better."

"Patsy won't be going in either," Mr. Lane went on, "your mother and I discussed it with the Leighs last night, so I expect Patsy will be round this morning and you can keep each other company." Carol nodded listlessly. The telephone rang. Her father went to answer it.

"That was the local southern television centre. They want to come and film a news item for the evening news." Mrs. Lane and Carol stared at each other.

"Gracious!" Carol exclaimed, "you mean we might be on television?"

"I expect it will depend on what else comes up today that might be more newsworthy, but it would be wonderful publicity," her mother said.

It was a strangely unreal day. Patsy came over after breakfast. Her father had said he had important business and had disappeared in the car.

"Something must be up. There was a kind of mystery about Dad driving off like that." Patsy kicked the gravel with her foot. "What are we going to do all day without the ponies?" The two girls wandered aimlessly across the lawn, ending up leaning on the paddock gate, staring at its emptiness. A car drove up and stopped beside them and a young man wound the window down.

"Hallo," he said, "Are you Carol Lane?" Carol nodded. "Will you tell me about your missing ponies? I'm a reporter from the Evening News." He held out an identity card.

"Come into the house," a voice said from behind him. The reporter and the girls jumped. They hadn't seen Mr. Lane come across the lawn. "We need all the help and publicity we can get," he explained. "Come into the house and my wife will make you a coffee."

Much later in the day after watching themselves on TV the girls sat slumped in comfy chairs in the lounge.

"It's odd seeing ourselves on the screen, isn't it?" Patsy looked at Carol. "We were wondering what we would do all day, but it's been hectic, hasn't it?" Carol nodded wearily.

"I feel shattered," she remarked. "I just hope all the talking and publicity will do some good, so far there doesn't seem to be any sign of the ponies anywhere. I really haven't enjoyed today at all."

"I'm not looking forward to school tomorrow, are you? I expect everyone will want to know what's happened, and I don't want to talk about it any more."

"I wonder where your Dad went?" Carol said thoughtfully. "He doesn't usually leave the parish during the week does he?" Patsy shook her head.

There was no news of the ponies the next morning, but when the two girls met to go to school Patsy explained where her father had gone.

"He knew the Smiths wouldn't cope with police questioning, and that police generally have so much trouble with travellers they are often not sympathetic, so he drove to the Cotswolds to find them."

"Did he?" Carol asked. "It was good of him to go."

"Yes, he got there about half an hour after the police. The police had seen there were two piebald ponies tethered by the caravan, and were convinced they'd found Pinto and Paddy. Daddy was able to persuade them that they weren't our ponies."

"No, of course, one would have been Pinto's mother, and the other her most recent foal." Carol exclaimed.

"That's right, and Dad told the gypsies that we had never suspected them at all. He said Reuban and Mrs. Smith had been really upset, thinking we had sent the police."

"How awful!" Carol was horrified, "they don't think that now, do they?"

"No, and Mrs. Smith sent us a message. She told Dad to tell us that joy follows sorrow and after one for silver we will have two for gold."

"What on earth does that mean?" Carol looked puzzled.

"Well, I hope the joy following sorrow bit means we'll get the ponies back, but the one for silver two for gold has me baffled."

School wasn't as bad as the girls had feared, but at the end of the day, and later by the end of the week, there was still no news of the ponies. There had been one or two moments when sighting of piebald ponies were reported, but they all turned out to be false hopes.

The week dragged by, and the next one too. Mr. and Mrs. Lane cancelled the entries for the BDS Show at Smiths Lawn.

"If we do get the ponies back now they are not likely to be fit enough to compete at that standard." Mrs. Lane said sadly.

Carol and Patsy thought every day that passed it seemed less likely that their beloved ponies would be found. They were doing their end of term exams, and both of them found it hard to concentrate.

"I'm dreading exam results this term." Patsy confided to Carol as they came out of the classroom after the history exam. "I know I haven't done well. I just didn't feel like revising, and I couldn't answer half the questions."

Their parents and the Roberts family were still working hard to try and find the ponies, checking every sale and every market, driving miles each week to see possible Paddys and Pintos that people had reported seeing. No one dared voice the fact that it looked as if the ponies would never be found. The thought was too ghastly to contemplate.

"Hull!" Mr. Lane exclaimed, coming back from the telephone,

the second Saturday since the ponies disappeared. "I ask you, Hull, of all places! A farmer has telephoned to say two piebald ponies have appeared in one of his fields, and could they be ours? It's miles to drive and I expect it will be another wild goose chase. Is it worth the bother?" Mrs. Lane looked at him with sympathy.

"Will you go?" she asked, "you must be getting very tired." Mr. Lane had taken his annual three weeks holiday, he had been so determined to find the ponies. They had got marvellous publicity but such a lot of false sightings. It was amazing how many piebald ponies there were in the country.

He couldn't bear to see Carol becoming paler and quieter every day, and Patsy without her cheery sparkle was just not like Patsy at all.

"I think I must," he said wearily. "I'll leave straight away, it will take at least four to five hours to get to Hull, and then I've got to find the farm. I'll find somewhere to stay overnight and come back tomorrow. I'll 'phone as soon as I have any news."

Soon after he had left the 'phone rang, and it was Ian from the Magpie Carriage Driving Centre.

"Ann and I were so sorry to hear your news," he said, "and Liz has told us you still haven't heard anything. We wondered if it would give the girls something else to think about if you brought them over here for the day. It might help them take their minds off their problems for a little while. Tell Carol we would take them pair driving, Liz said that is something Carol is very keen to do."

"You are kind!" Mrs. Lane exclaimed. "I think that would do them both so much good. I'll go and ask them and 'phone you back."

CHAPTER IX

The Magpie Carriage Driving Centre was an exciting place to be. Carol and Patsy were welcomed by Ann and Ian and told to go and find their way around for a while because they were both teaching.

"Can we watch?" Patsy asked.

"You can if you're quiet." Ann smiled , "I'm teaching in our manege over there," she pointed beyond the stables, "but Ian is taking Jacob out for a drive, so you will only see them set off."

Jacob turned out to be a teenage boy who obviously wasn't too keen on being observed. He looked very unfriendly and didn't even say hallo to the girls as they stood watching them get ready. Ian brought out a bay cob of about 14.2hh and between them they harnessed him and put him to an exercise cart. Jacob took up the reins and got in. He nodded to Ian, who let go of the cob's head and came round to sit beside Jacob. They set off down the drive with the cob wandering rather, and Jacob with slack reins, leaning forward rather nervously. Ian was talking quietly to him as they disappeared out of sight.

"He looked as if he was a beginner," Carol said as they watched them go down the drive, "perhaps that's why he didn't want us watching him. It's a bit off putting when you're not very confident."

"He wasn't very friendly, was he?" Patsy dismissed Jacob. "Let's go and see the tack room."

The tack room was impressive, with rows of collars and harness of all kinds hung neatly round the walls. There was a lovely smell of clean leather and rows and rows of rosettes pinned on boards running round the room just below the ceiling.

"Wow!" exclaimed Carol, "what an enormous number of rosettes, and some of them are rather grand." They spent a few minutes trying to see where they had been won, but they were so high up that it was difficult.

"Let's go and watch Ann teaching." Patsy had itchy feet. She peered through the next door. "This is only the feed store, I'd rather see the horses or see Ann teach."

"OK," Carol said, "let's look in all the stables on the way to the manege." To their disappointment most of the stables were empty. There were only three occupied. The first one had a black pony mare inside, which was being groomed by a girl. She smiled at the girls.

"Hi, I'm Alison, are you Carol and Patsy?" The girls nodded. "This is Magic," she went on, "I'm getting her ready for you to drive."

"What's she like?" Carol asked.

"She's not a beginners pony. Have you done quite a lot of driving?"

"We have got ponies of our own," Carol said cautiously, "or at least we had," she added sadly. Alison looked puzzled.

"I don't understand." Patsy took over the story.

"Our ponies have been stolen. It has been absolutely awful. They've been missing for two weeks now, and we might never get them back."

"I thought you looked familiar, but I couldn't think why," Alison exclaimed, "I saw you on television just after they vanished. How absolutely ghastly. I do hope they turn up."

"Thanks," Carol didn't want to talk about it any more. "We're just going to watch Ann teaching."

"You'll enjoy that, she's a super teacher," Alison's face lit up. "I've only been here for six months, but I've learnt such a lot, Ann and Ian are great to work for."

There were two other ponies in stables, a pair of grey Welsh section A's who were very alike.

"I expect they are the pair that we are going to see driven," Carol said hopefully. "They look rather sweet." They stroked the ponies noses over the doors, and then made their way to the manege.

The lady that Ann was teaching was obviously not a beginner, she looked very competent and experienced.

"They're very fussy," Carol was watching critically. "Look, Ann is adjusting the angle of her whip and making her sit slightly differently." When the turnout set off round the manege the chestnut mare moved beautifully.

"What a super pony," Patsy leant on the rails at the side of the manege.

"Mm," Carol was watching the lady driving. "She drives well, look at her lovely supple wrists." They were content to stay until the lesson ended, it was fascinating. As the lady drove the chestnut back to the stables, Ann called to the girls.

"We'll get a pony for you in a minute."

It was fun driving a new pony. Carol and Patsy took Magic down to the manege accompanied by Ann and Alison. Ann stood in the manege giving Carol some useful advice while Alison leant on the rails and watched, but not for long.

"Could you come and help me set up cones, please?" Ann asked, and Alison came in to give a hand. Patsy jumped off the backstep to help as well. Carol was finding Magic slower to respond than their ponies or Harmony. "Use your whip as a guide to send Magic right or left," Ann called, "it will push her on as well. Don't hit her, just imagine the whip is the leg you would use if you were riding." It was surprising what a difference that made. The time flew by, and Carol was feeling really at home with Magic by the time they finished and brought her back to the yard. Carol looked at Patsy.

"I almost feel guilty because it's been fun," she said. Patsy nodded.

"I know, I almost forgot for a few minutes and then I felt that awful blank feeling again."

Alison held Magic while Patsy hopped down and fetched Carol's crutches which were leaning against the stable wall. Carol didn't offer to help unharness, because Alison was there with Patsy and she wasn't sure how Magic would react to her crutches when she saw them.

As she moved away Ian came to the door of the house and called. "Telephone for you and Patsy." They made their way to the house, rather surprised. A thousand possibilities crossed Carol's mind as Patsy dashed to the 'phone. Carol hardly dared to look at her. Was it good news or bad? Patsy turned and handed the 'phone to Carol.

"It's your father," she said, her voice wobbling. She threw herself into Ann's arms and burst into tears. "He's found them!" she sobbed, "he's found them. Paddy and Pinto are all right." Carol listened intently for several minutes before putting the 'phone down looking slightly dazed. She sat down rather heavily on the nearby chair.

"It's over, we're going to get them back." Then she looked at Patsy, and got up again to go over to her. "What are you crying for, you silly thing! It's wonderful news. Paddy and Pinto are coming home!" Her voice crackled with excitement.

"I think I'm crying with relief and happiness," Patsy pulled herself away from Ann looking rather embarrassed. "I'm sorry to be such a fool, but it was just the shock, after all these days of waiting."

"Come into the kitchen and tell us what your father had to say, while I get lunch out of the oven. Call Alison and Jacob please, or Carol will have to tell her story twice." Ian called from the door, and Ann took a big casserole dish and jacket potatoes out of the cooker.

"Where's Jacob?" Ann asked as Alison burst into the room. "I told his mother I'd do lunch for him as well."

"He's coming," Alison pulled a chair out and sat down. "What's happened?" Carol was just about to speak when she saw Jacob hovering uncertainly in the doorway.

"Come and join us," she cried. "Patsy and I have had some wonderful news which we want to share with everyone."

"Yes, come in Jacob." Ian said encouragingly. The boy moved almost reluctantly to a chair and sat down. "You probably don't know that Carol and Patsy had their ponies stolen a fortnight ago and they have been desperately searching for them. Carol's father was told of two piebald ponies who had turned up in a field on the outskirts of Hull, so he drove up to see them. Now, Carol," he turned to her smiling. "Tell us what your father had to say."

"He found the place quite easily," Carol explained. "The man is a Mr. Hopkins, and he has a small farm just outside Hull. He gave Daddy good directions. When he got there, he and Mr. Hopkins went straight to this field quite close to the sea, and Pinto and Paddy were happily grazing. Daddy said he couldn't believe his eyes. The ponies whinnied when he called and came over. Apparently they look a bit fat and unkempt but otherwise they're fine. Daddy thinks that all the publicity, and the fact that they are both freeze branded made them too hot for the thieves to handle, so they dumped them!" She stopped, and her face lit up. "Isn't it wonderful? I can hardly believe it. The best news of all is that they are coming back by lorry tomorrow!"

51

CHAPTER X

Lunch was such a happy meal and afterwards Ann took the two girls to the tack room where they collected a set of pairs harness. Alison and Patsy brought the two grey ponies out of their stables and tied them to rings in the wall, while Ann pulled out a modern four wheel vehicle with a central pole.

"These ponies are called Murray and Mint," she explained. "Alison has Mint and Patsy is tying up Murray. When you start to look for a pair to go together, what do you think is important?"

"They should match?" Patsy asked.

"Yes, but what do you mean by 'match'?" Ann queried.

"They should be the same height because then they would look even, and have matching paces," Carol suggested.

"And be the same colour too, like Murray and Mint. That looks nice," Patsy added, "but I'm not sure how much that matters."

"It matters if you are going to show them, then the more alike they are the better, ideally they should look like one pony from the side view. Murray and Mint are full brothers, Murray is a year younger than Mint but we bought them together from the same stud where they were born." Ann turned to the vehicle, "Let's look at this for a moment. The obvious difference is that there are no shafts, the ponies stand each side of a pole which acts as a guide and as the vehicle's braking power." Ann turned and picked up one set of harness, while Alison collected the other set. "This is traditional harness and the collar goes on first the same way as you would put it on for a single, upside down and then gently turned round into position. The hames are fastened up with the hame straps, but they are buckled with the points of the straps facing inwards." Patsy looked puzzled and Ann caught her glance. "This is in case of an accident when in order to get the horses out quickly it is easier to undo the hame strap than to try and release a trace. At the bottom of the collar the hame straps are joined by a kidney-shaped link and loose on this is a ring . The pole strap or pole chain is clipped onto this ring." As Ann spoke she was putting the collar on Murray while Alison did the same with Mint. "The false martingale is buckled round the bottom of the collar, through the kidney link and this secures the hames onto the collar.

When the pole so many straps. Anyway moves it causes pressure on the hames, especially when the ponies are going down a hill or if they are being pulled up. The false martingale aids stability and prevents the collar from moving."

Carol and Patsy were trying to look intelligent and remember it all, but there were several differences to single harness. Carol remembered how baffled she had felt when Liz first showed her how to harness Harmony. There seemed now the moment had come to do the one thing Carol had been really keen to do she found she couldn't concentrate. Her heart kept singing 'the ponies are found, they'll be back home tomorrow' so loudly she felt everyone should be able to hear. She looked across at Patsy who caught her eye and grinned broadly. The sun was warm on their backs and suddenly it was a wonderful day.

With a start Carol realised Ann had put on the rest of the harness and she hadn't taken in a thing. She tried to concentrate. Patsy ran her hand through her hair.

"It seems awfully complicated," she looked rather baffled.

"No, it's not really," Ann laughed. "Don't worry about it today, just remember what you can and enjoy the drive. When you come to junior whip camp we'll make you harness them up and put to several times. That's the best way to learn."

When the ponies were both harnessed they were stood, one each side of the pole. Ann and Alison clipped the pole chains to the floating ring on the kidney links on each collar, and the outside trace was fastened into place.

"Now with each pony held into place by the pole chain and the outside trace they can't move away from the pole. This is the only safe way to put to. To fit the inside trace next you have to lean behind the pony, so you don't want a bad tempered pony who might kick. Pair harness with a collar doesn't have to have breeching, so you have a trace carrier to stop the traces sagging. If the traces sag the pony could put a leg over with disastrous results." Ann fitted the reins, the inner coupling rein first and then the draught or outside rein.

"Do you know I'd never noticed that the reins cross!" Carol exclaimed in surprise.

"Oh yes, the whip still only holds two reins, but about two feet from her hands the reins divide, the outside draught rein goes to

53

the outside bit ring, but the inside coupling reins cross, the left hand coupling rein going to the inside of the right hand pony's bit and the right hand coupling rein going to the left hand pony's bit. It's correct to call the ponies, Mint on the left the nearside pony, and Murray on the right is the offside pony." Carol and Patsy thought it was very strange but neither of them felt like asking any more questions, their brains were already baffled.

Ann mounted the vehicle, Alison was stood at the ponies' heads. Patsy helped Carol up to sit next to Ann and then hopped up behind to sit on a little seat at one side.

"Are you ready?" Ann asked, and when the girls nodded she asked Alison to stand aside and gave the command to walk on. Alison stepped up and sat down opposite Patsy as they moved off.

It was an exhilarating drive. Carol watched fascinated as Ann kept the pair together, explaining how Murray was keener than Mint, so she had to make sure Mint did his share of the work. She showed Carol how to loop a rein to turn corners and how to watch the pole moving as well as keeping an eagle eye on the two ponies. Carol was filled with the desire to drive Paddy and Pinto like this. When Ann pulled the ponies up, and suggested that Carol drove them home, she nearly burst with surpressed excitement. Alison went to their heads as Ann got down and Carol edged her way across to the driving seat. With Ann back beside her she proudly gave the command to walk on.

They only walked the last half mile home, mainly to cool the ponies off, but Carol's cup of happiness completely overflowed as she turned them into the carriage driving centre and saw her mother with Mrs. Leigh who had come to collect them. It was hard to sit quietly on her seat and wait for everyone else to do the work and help her down. She wished she could leap lightly to the ground and run to tell her mother how thrilled she was to have their beloved ponies coming back home. She waved frantically. Alison jumped down to hold the ponies, Patsy quickly followed and ran across to the car.

"Isn't it wonderful?" she cried excitely. "Carol and I are so thrilled. I don't think we can quite believe it." Mrs. Leigh smiled as she got out of the car.

"We are feeling like that," she said giving Patsy a hug, "but it really is true." She looked across to the grey ponies. "Have you and Carol enjoyed your day?" Patsy nodded.

"It's been a bit strange somehow. This morning was fun, but we both felt a bit guilty enjoying ourselves. Since Carol's father 'phoned we've just been over the moon." Mrs. Lane walked over to Carol to help her down.

"Good old Daddy." Carol said happily as she propped herself on her crutches. She smiled rather mistily at her mother. "Everyone has worked so hard to find them. It's just brilliant to think they'll be home tomorrow."

Ann and Alison put Murray and Mint back in the stables, and Carol and Patsy went over to say good-bye.

"Thanks for having us. We've had a super day, and driving with Murray and Mint was just fabulous." Ann smiled.

"Not long to camp now. We shall look forward to having you both. We are all so pleased that everything has turned out well after all." Later, on the way home, Patsy turned to Carol.

"I've been thinking," she said, "about Mrs. Smith's message, one for silver could be the cup at Windsor and the joy following sorrow bit has come true now we've got the ponies back. The only thing missing is the two for gold. Do you think it could be to do with driving the ponies as a pair?"

Carol looked thoughtful. "I suppose it might be, but I don't see any gold on the horizon at the moment!"

CHAPTER XI

To their annoyance Carol and Patsy had to go to school on Monday. No amount of pleading had made their parents give way. The day dragged. It seemed as if the end of the last lesson would never come. At last they were free to collect up their books and make their way to where Mrs. Lane was waiting with the car.

"Yes, they are home safely." Mrs. Lane answered their anxious questions. "They're back in the paddock and they're fine." As the car turned into the drive Carol and Patsy's hearts were thumping and they both felt choked with emotion. They could hardly believe their eyes. It just looked as if the ponies had never been away. They were grazing happily. The girls got out by the gate and called. It was a wonderful moment as they stroked the familiar noses and patted their necks.

"They are fat!" Carol exclaimed. "At least nobody has starved them. I wonder what has happened to them in the two weeks they've been missing."

"We'll never know." Her mother replied. "I think we'll restrict their grass for a few days, we don't want them to get laminitis. They will soon slim down with a little work and less grazing."

A few days after the ponies return when things were getting back to normal, the telephone rang. Mrs. Lane went to answer it and quite a time elapsed before she returned to the kitchen. Carol looked up from the table where she was peeling potatoes for supper.

"Who was it? she asked. Her mother was looking very thoughtful.

"It was Ian from the driving centre."

"What did he want?" Carol was curious.

"Apparently you told Ann it was your great ambition to drive Paddy and Pinto as a pair?" Carol nodded.

"Mm, I've wanted to do that ever since we got Paddy, but I didn't see how, and anyway we have only just discovered how good and quiet Paddy is. We've only had him since our holiday at Easter. It's my dream really, and it was fantastic driving Murray and Mint the other day." Her face lit up as she spoke. "Anyway what's that got to do with Ian 'phoning?"

"I shall have to speak to your father," her mother said almost to herself.

"Oh, come on, Mummy! What's it all about?" Carol was impatient to know.

"Well, you mustn't get too excited, Carol, because your father may say it's too expensive. Ian and Ann have offered to have Paddy and Pinto to try them together as a pair. They have offered a discounted rate, and suggested if we agree, that the ponies could go over there the week before camp. Then we could take you and Patsy over a couple of times, and if Paddy and Pinto take to pair driving you could drive them under instruction for the week of camp."

"Oh, Mummy!" Carol could hardly believe her ears. "Do you think Daddy will agree? Could it be my birthday present? My birthday's in August. I could have it in advance. Is it terribly expensive? Could it be my birthday and Christmas presents? I'd do anything to learn to drive a pair properly." She was so excited, all her words came out in a rush. "When will Daddy be back from work? He's not going to be late tonight, is he?"

"Steady on, Carol," her mother interrupted the flow. "I didn't realise quite how much you wanted to drive the ponies as a pair! I don't want to disappoint you so don't expect too much until I've spoken to Daddy. I can't promise anything."

Her father was late, and when Carol tried to ring Patsy at the vicarage there was no reply. She wandered about, looking out of the window to watch for her father. Then eventually she returned to the 'phone and dialed the Roberts telephone number. This time she was lucky.

"Hallo." Liz had picked up the 'phone.

"Liz! I didn't think I'd get you. Have you broken up already?" Carol was surprised. "I'm so glad you're there to talk to." She poured out everything that had happened at the carriage driving centre, and what had followed from that. Usually she, Liz and Patsy kept in regular touch with each other, but the last two weeks had been so hectic, plus the fact that it was difficult to get Liz on the 'phones at boarding school, they always seemed to be engaged. Suddenly she heard the front door close, which meant her father was back from work. "I'll ring you back later, Liz. Daddy has just come in and I must go." She had been balancing on one crutch, so she picked up the other one and made her way to join her parents.

Her father needed quite a lot of convincing that this proposition was a good idea. Carol pulled out all her powers of persuasion and in the end her father agreed.

"It will have to be your birthday and Christmas present," he said firmly, "so when Christmas comes and you've forgotten about the summer holidays you mustn't expect anything big, just your stocking."

"I don't mind, Daddy, really I don't. This will be the most wonderful present since I started driving." Carol flung her arms round her father and gave him a big hug. "Thank you, thank you," she cried.

Term ended, and Patsy and Carol's worst fears were realised when their exam results raised unfavourable comments in their end of term reports. Despite this the summer holidays stretched ahead full of the promise of exciting things to do. There was only a week before Pinto and Paddy went to the driving centre. The girls were determined the ponies were going to look well and do them justice. They worked hard, driving both ponies every day and grooming them until they shone. They were beginning to lose the fat they had put on while they were on unlimited grass in Hull, and looked quite streamlined again.

When the day came to box them up and take them to the driving centre Carol found she had mixed feelings. She was so keen to get them going as a pair, yet they had only had the ponies back for such a short while. As she watched her mother and Patsy load them into the horsebox she had sudden doubts.

I mustn't be stupid, she thought, they are going to a super place. Patsy slipped out of the box door and came across.

"What are you looking so thoughtful about?" she asked, and Carol started.

"Nothing," she shook off her feelings of doubt, "I was miles away. Are we ready to go?" Her mother pushed the iron rail across the back of the ramp to keep the ponies in, then she stood back.

"Yes, let's get you both aboard. I wish the driving centre wasn't quite so far away. It would be much more convenient if it was ten minutes down the road, instead of forty miles. We have

58

been going over there quite a lot recently, and it is quite time consuming driving to and fro."

Ann and Ian hadn't seen the ponies together before.

"Oh, they're lovely!" Ann cried as Patsy led Pinto down the ramp, followed by Mrs. Lane with Paddy. Carol's heart swelled with pride. Ann's enthusiasm was so genuine. The two ponies stood side by side, heads alert, ears pricked as they took in their new surroundings. They did look very smart. She moved across on her crutches to stand by Paddy. The little pony stood steady as a rock while Carol made a fuss of him.

"They're easy to tell apart." She smiled at Ann and Ian. "Pinto has the tidy mane while Paddy's mane bounces about and never lies flat. We've tried leaving it plaited for two or three days and it looks great for about a couple of hours, then it's back to its normal wayward state! Paddy has more black on him than Pinto as well." Patsy interrupted her.

"Pinto was given to Daddy by the gypsies." She said proudly. "He did them a good turn and they gave him Pinto for my brothers and me." She grinned. "Luckily the twins aren't interested in ponies any more. He was just a pet until I met Carol who had started driving with Liz Roberts. When the gypsies next came to stay in our orchard Reuban told us that Pinto was a driving pony and that's how it all started." Ian was looking carefully at the pair.

"I think I shall know which is which," he said. "So Pinto is the most experienced, is he?"

"We've had him longest," Carol agreed. "We've only had Paddy since the end of the Easter hols, but he's ever so quiet and steady." As she spoke Alison appeared round the corner of the stables wheeling a barrow.

"Wow, what fun!" She exclaimed. She put the barrow down and came over. "Aren't they super? So these are your ponies that were stolen! You were lucky to get them back." Carol and Patsy smiled happily. It was lovely to have their beloved ponies so admired.

"We'll put them in adjacent stables, so they can see each other for the moment." Ian said, "while we go into the house and write down their home routine and what you feed them. They'll settle more quickly on a familiar routine."

"Are you going to try them together today?" Carol asked

eagerly. "Could we stay and watch?"

"No," Ann said firmly, "they seem very steady and reliable, but we must let them settle in. We'll take them slowly at first, because they have to get used to us as well. We'll ring you in a couple of days time if we have any news."

They left the ponies in the stables when they returned to their horsebox, and climbed in. As Mrs. Lane drove down the drive the two girls waved good-bye.

"It's only a week." Patsy said, looking at Carol's face.

"I know, but I wish we could be there to help and tell Ann and Ian all about their funny little ways." Her mother laughed.

"Don't worry, Carol. Ann and Ian have lots of experience, and if they're worried they can always 'phone us."

"And then it's the junior camp." Patsy reminded her. They had been sent details of the camp in the post, and it certainly looked as if they were going to have an action packed week. There were going to be instruction, competitions, barbecues and a disco besides the chance to work for the BDS exams.

"I was going to do lots of preparation for the exam," Carol said, "but with the ponies being stolen I'd forgotten all about it."

"Why not do some this week, while you haven't got the ponies to look after and drive?" Her mother suggested sensibly. Patsy's face fell.

"Boring!" She cried. "We've only just finished school exams. I don't feel like doing any more swotting." Carol looked thoughtful.

"I might just look at the syllabus and remind myself of what it covers." Patsy grimaced.

"I don't want to know. I just want to have fun at camp, not be fretting over exams all week. It will spoil everything having to worry about another beastly exam!"

60

Every time the telephone rang Carol hoped it would be Ann or Ian, but two days passed and they heard nothing. Mrs. Lane got rather fed up with the girls hanging around the house, so the second day she took them into Mossminster and dropped them off at the cinema while she did some shopping. The film was disappointing, but at least it gave Carol and Patsy something else to talk about.

The 'phone was ringing when they opened the door of Old Chimneys on their return. Patsy dashed to pick it up for Carol.

"Hi. No, nothing, not a word!" She said, and turning to face Carol, she mouthed "It's Liz". She spoke back into the 'phone. "Yes, I expect so, I'll see what Carol says." She looked at Carol, "Liz says when we go over to see Pinto and Paddy can she come to?"

"Good idea," Carol nodded, "it's about time we all got together, now it's the holidays. Tell Liz we'll ring her as soon as we get any news."

It was not until late in the evening and Patsy had gone home when Ian telephoned, but even then he didn't tell them much. Mrs. Lane answered the call, and told Carol afterwards that Ian had just said they could go over tomorrow if they liked.

"Didn't he say anything? Not how they were getting on, or how they were settling, and whether they had tried them together?" Carol could have cried with sheer frustration. "Mummy, why didn't you ask?"

"Well darling, he was in a hurry and you'll know tomorrow. It's not long to wait."

"When are we going?" Carol hoped it would be in the morning.

"I've arranged to be there at eleven o'clock, and we can take Patsy and collect Liz on the way. I've said that we'll take a picnic lunch."

"Are you going to stay too?" Carol was surprised.

"I'm interested in Paddy and Pinto's progress as well, you know! I thought I'd ask Mrs. Roberts if she'd like to keep me company. We can see how the ponies are getting on, have our picnic and come home. You had better ring Patsy first and I'll ring the Roberts."

Carol woke very early the next morning. She lay in bed wondering how the ponies had been behaving. It was only half past six, but she felt wide awake. Suddenly she decided to get up. When she looked out of the window it was one of those glorious early summer mornings. She took her crutches, made her way to the front door and quietly opened it.

Outside the air was fresh and the lawn sparkled with the dew. The sun was already shining and everywhere seemed soft, misty and warm. Carol made her way to the garden seat under the copper beech tree on the lawn, but the seat was wet with dew. She crossed the lawn, leaving dark footprints in the drenched grass, she could feel the dew soaking her shoes. Leaning on the paddock gate she took in deep breaths of air as she looked at the familiar scene, and thought about the day ahead. She did so hope everything had gone smoothly. It would be so disappointing if the ponies didn't get on together as a pair, but she couldn't see why they shouldn't, after all they were friends and shared the same paddock at home.

Her thoughts were rudely interrupted as Pip and Squeak appeared, racing across the lawn barking until they realised who it was leaning on the gate. Then they stopped momentarily, before wriggling their sturdy little bodies in delight and flinging themselves at her feet. Carol reached down and patted each in turn.

"Someone else is up," she said to the dogs, "I could eat some breakfast." It was such a beautiful morning that they took their breakfast outside. The sun was already warm and there was all the promise of a glorious day.

Patsy was waiting for them by the vicarage gate, in a bright yellow tee-shirt and denim shorts. She waved gaily and ran to get into the car.

"Isn't this exciting?" she cried, putting the box with her sandwiches on the seat beside her and clipping on her seat belt. "What a fabulous day!" The eight mile drive to the Roberts house flew by in a burble of excited chatter. Mrs. Roberts and Liz were waiting too, so the car was quickly speeding on its way again. As they neared the driving centre Carol thought how awful it would be if they were told the ponies were not going to be any good.

There was such an air of optimism in the car.

Ian fended off their excited questions when they arrived. "You must come and see," was all he would say. Ann was smiling as she led Paddy over to tie up by the wall next to Pinto. Patsy and Carol made a great fuss of both ponies. "It's only two days!" Ann laughed.

"Yes, but we'd only just got them home and it seemed strange to be without them again." Patsy turned to explain, her arms round Pinto's neck.

"Please tell us!" Carol pleaded, rubbing Paddy's forehead. "They are going to be all right, aren't they?" Ann nodded and gave in.

"Yes," she said, "we don't want to raise your hopes too much, but we're very pleased with them." Carol's sense of relief was enormous. She grinned happily at Patsy and Liz.

Ann and Ian made the two girls talk them all through harnessing, while Liz and the two mothers watched carefully. Alison and Jacob appeared, pulling the carriage out into the yard.

"This is Alison, who is working here, and Jacob is staying with us for a few weeks." She explained to Mrs. Roberts and Liz. Alison looked up and smiled. "Hi," she said. "I think you'll be pleased with your two." Jacob nodded at the girls shyly. His dark hair flopped untidily across his rather sad, withdrawn face.

"Who's going to help Patsy put them to the carriage?" Ann looked at Liz. "I expect you'd like to, wouldn't you?" Liz nodded eagerly.

"I'll do Paddy for Carol, if you tell me what to do." She moved to Paddy's head and held him.

"We're going to put Pinto on the offside of the pole and Paddy on the nearside," Ian explained. "We've tried them on both sides, but this seems to suit them best. It is good if you can alternate them, so they will go either side, but for today we'll have Pinto on the offside." Patsy and Liz led the ponies into position and held them quietly while Ann and Alison did up the pole chains, then the outside traces followed by the inside ones, and coupled up the reins. "By the way, there are two of you holding the ponies today, but if you only have one groom it is very important to stand on one side of the pole. If you stand in the middle in front of that pole, and the ponies jump forward you could have a very nasty

63

injury from it." Patsy and Liz grinned at each other and carefully stood directly in front of their pony's head, away from the pole. "We're going to drive them in the manege," Ian explained, "so you can see more easily how they are getting on."

Carol stood watching happily. This seemed to be more than she had dared to dream about. Ann took the reins and got into the carriage, Alison hopped in too. When Ann had picked up her whip and settled herself she nodded to Patsy and Liz.

"You can let go now," she said. "Pinto, Paddy, walk on!" The two ponies moved forward. Pinto was definitely quicker off the mark, and Ann spoke to Paddy, "Paddy, pull on," as they went towards the manege. Carol's eyes were shining as she started off on her crutches following them. She hardly heard Ian talking to her mother and Mrs. Roberts. She was gazing in pride at the ponies.

"Pinto wants to do all the work," Ian was explaining. "It's not that Paddy is particularly lazy. It is just that he is not so forward going. They have to learn to pull together at. At the moment they are a bit ragged and uneven. It is important that Paddy is not allowed to let Pinto do the work or he will quickly discover that it is far easier to stay back and be a passenger! They are doing really well. We just didn't know what to expect. It is easy to assume that as they both drive well as singles and know each other they will go as a pair, but it is never wise to assume anything with horses!" He laughed, "however at the moment we are very pleased."

"What's wrong with your legs?" Jacob spoke quietly from behind Carol and she started. She hadn't noticed him come up behind her where she was leaning on the manege rails.

"I was in a car accident," she said briefly. "About three years ago. I'll never get any better, but I manage." She pulled her eyes away from the ponies to look at the boy beside her. "Why are you staying here, are you on a course or something?" she countered. His rather long, narrow face was sad.

"My father's had a heart by-pass operation." He looked down at his feet. "It's easier for mother if I'm out of the way at the moment, because she spends all day at the hospital. So Ann and Ian have me here."

"I'm sorry." Carol's heart was touched. No wonder he had seemed distant and rather odd. "How awful to be foisted off while your father is ill. It must be difficult for you."

"It's hell." The dark eyes were sombre. "I just wanted you to know why I'm finding it difficult to join in. Of course I'm pleased about your ponies, but with Dad so ill, it doesn't seem important to me. I hope you'll understand." He looked rather pleadingly at Carol. "Could you tell the others, and just ask them not to mention it to me, because then I can cope. I don't want to talk about it." He moved away suddenly and leaned on the rails on his own.

Ann drove the ponies round the manege, changed diagonal and drove them the other way. Ian put out some cones, and Pinto and Paddy manoeuvred those quite neatly. It was not a polished performance but it was nice and calm. The onlookers watched for about ten minutes before Ann took the pair out of the manege and back to the stable yard. "Tomorrow we are going to take them along the road. We know they are good in traffic so it shouldn't be a problem." This time she and Alison held the ponies while Liz and Patsy learnt how to take them out of the vehicle safely. Then they led them off to graze in a paddock.

"If you want to come once more before camp, you can drive them yourself, Carol," Ann said over the picnic lunch in their garden. "They are such safe ponies that I think they will quickly improve." Carol's eyes shone.

"That would be brilliant," she cried. "Will I really be able to have a go myself?" Her mother looked worried.

"It's very early days," she said. "I would hate there to be an accident."

"I will sit beside Carol, and I can always take over if there is a problem." Ann reassured Mrs. Lane. "We shall be in the manege, which is safer as it is enclosed. I don't think we are rushing them. They have shown no signs of panic, they are sensible and Carol knows them so well."

CHAPTER XIII

The promise of that glorious day had been realised, Carol thought, sitting on the lawn the next day. The picnic had been such fun, sharing sandwiches in the warm June sunshine. She hadn't had the opportunity to tell the others about Jacob's father until they were driving home.

"Oh, poor boy," Mrs. Roberts had exclaimed. "I thought he seemed very quiet."

"He's still going to be staying there during junior camp." Carol added. "I think we'll have to try and be nice to him."

Carol picked up the stable management book she had been studying. It was hard to concentrate in this lovely weather she thought, but she was determined to pass her level one exam. She didn't think the driving side would be a problem, but she only had experience of their type of ponies, and had no idea, for example, about the merits or otherwise of shavings, peat or paper as alternatives to wheat straw for bedding. It was the same with feeding. She knew what her mother had always fed the ponies and why, but the options of other feeds she knew little about. It was making her think hard. Then she needed a knowledge of basic first aid. Road safety wasn't a problem as they had learnt that for the competition at Windsor over a year ago, but there was also minor veterinary knowledge, harness and vehicle care to mug up on. Carol smiled wryly to herself, the list seemed endless. Still because she wasn't able to be very physically active, she did have the time to study. She bent her head over her books again.

At the end of the week Carol and Patsy had gone back to the driving centre so Carol could drive Pinto and Paddy herself before camp began. It had been another very special day. The thrill of sitting behind both the ponies made her feel very elated. At first she had worried about the extra reins to the second pony, but she discovered that it was not so very different to driving a single. She was helped by the ponies because they were very responsive to her voice and their individual names. She found she could begin to give them orders separately and this was very exciting.

After her lesson Ann talked to Ian. "She's a natural driver you know, if she can get those ponies a little more polished, and responding really well to individual voice commands they will make a winning combination."

Packing for camp was quite fun. Mainly the girls would need jeans, shorts, shirts, jerseys and sensible shoes, but Carol was determined to put in one pretty skirt. She was collecting her boots when the 'phone rang and her mother called her.

"Darling, it's David, for you." Slightly surprised Carol picked up the 'phone.

"Hi, Carol, "David's deep voice sounded excited. "Your mother says you're packing for camp. So am I. Dad's got you that marathon strap, and I wondered if you'd like me to bring it to camp. We're sure to do some scurry driving and you could try it out."

"Oh that would be great, thank you David, and please thank your father for me."

"Right, I'll bring it then. See you tomorrow. Bye."

A few minutes later the 'phone rang again. Mrs. Lane picked it up. "It's for you again, Carol," she called.

"Who is it Mummy?" Carol made her way back to the 'phone.

"It's Jacob," her mother laughed, and handed the receiver over.

"Jacob?" Carol said with a query in her voice.

"Yes, Hallo Carol. It's Jacob. I've rung to find out if you are bringing your wheelchair to camp? I've had an idea, that's all, but I don't want to talk about it now. It just means you'll need your chair." Carol was completely mystified. What on earth could he want her to take her wheelchair for?

"Yes, I shall bring it. It saves my legs quite a lot."

"Good. See you tomorrow then." The 'phone went dead. Carol put the receiver down her end feeling really puzzled.

By the end of the evening the 'phone had rung twice more, once it was Patsy and then it was Liz. Mrs. Lane shook her head at her daughter. "At least it will be much quieter while you're away."

The driving centre was alive with activity when Carol and Patsy arrived the next day. It was strange, Carol thought, seeing so many other people unpacking, calling to each other and to Ian and Ann as if they were old friends. One or two looked curiously at Carol when she got out her crutches.

"I thought the disabled camp was next month," she heard a tall blonde girl say rather sarcastically to her companion as they watched Carol make her way towards the barn where the girls were sleeping. Oh dear, she thought, I hope it's not going to be difficult to be accepted. Then she forgot her worries as Liz and David appeared with their sleeping bags and waved. It helped having them to show she and Patsy what to do, and even Jacob became a friendly face among so many strangers.

By the evening Carol was shattered. They had been kept very busy indeed and it had been great fun. She and Patsy had decided they wouldn't say anything about Paddy and Pinto yet as they guessed none of the others would have brought their own ponies. They managed to sneak off after tea and were delighted when the little piebalds were pleased to see them.

"Have you seen the programme for the week, pinned up on the wall?" Patsy asked as they made their way back to the main yard. "We seem to be split into different groups each day. I thought we might be with Liz and David, but we're not with them all the time. I think it's a shame." The blonde girl appeared round a corner. Carol had discovered that her name was Sadie.

"Having a sneaky preview to try and spot the good ponies?" she asked, "That's a bit sly. I'm going to drive a pair this week. Ian promised I could. I drive pairs for my father." She looked at Carol. "How did you get into camp?" She asked. Patsy was furious at her patronizing tone.

"Ian and Ann watched Carol win her class at the Windsor Horse Show," she retorted. "They thought she was good enough to come."

"Shut up, Patsy," Carol said quickly.

"My, what a little firebrand." Sadie laughed unpleasantly. "Still I suppose your minder has to earn her keep!" She turned sharply and walked off.

"What a cow!" Patsy stared after her. "How could she be so beastly?" Carol felt quite shaken.

"I can't understand why she's picked on me," she said slowly. "It doesn't make sense."

"You'll be late for supper. Have you both been struck by lightning?" The two girls jumped as Jacob appeared from behind them. Then his face changed. "What's the matter, you look upset? The ponies are O.K. aren't they? I saw them earlier." Carol tried to pull herself together.

"It's nothing really, Jacob. The tall blonde girl was a bit odd just now, that's all."

"Odd!" Patsy exclaimed, "she was just plain beastly." Carol shot her a warning look.

"Was it Sadie?" Jacob asked and Patsy nodded. "Her father's important in the driving world. He has some super horses and he's nice, but Sadie thinks she knows it all. I bet she was beastly to you because there's been a bit of talk that you were coming because you were so good. I expect she's rattled in case you are better than her."

"But that's silly!" Carol exclaimed. " There must be others here much better than me, and I'm disabled anyway. I can't be a threat. Where did the rumours come from?"

"I don't know. Come on," Jacob changed the subject quickly, "we won't get any supper if you don't get a move on."

Liz and David had kept places for them at supper and Jacob squeezed in as well. Only two, besides Liz and David, had been at the earlier camp, and Liz pointed them out.

"There's Helen, with fair hair, and Andrew, the rather plump boy sitting next to her. They were fun." Liz introduced them after supper and Carol found they were very friendly. She had the chance to say to Patsy to keep calm and not mention Sadie at all. "Don't let her see we're bothered," she said. "We don't want to create an atmosphere. We'll just keep out of her way."

Carol's legs were aching by the time everyone headed for sleeping bags at the end of the day. They were still tired when she got dressed the next morning so she went across to breakfast in her wheelchair. Most of the first day was spent going through all the basics of carriage driving to find out and assess how much each person had done. Everyone had a turn to drive either in the manege or a field . Paddy and Pinto were not mentioned and stayed out in their paddock.

At lunchtime the atmosphere was much more relaxed as they chatted among themselves. Patsy too, had driven one of the grey ponies, Murray.

"I just groom for Carol." She had protested when Ann told her she was going to drive.

"You'll be a much better groom if you can drive as well. Also if

69

there was an emergency you would be of far more use." Ann told her firmly. Alison came to be back step groom for Patsy while Carol sat on a bench outside the manege and watched. Helen and Andrew were there too, taking it in turns to drive or groom with Mint. When Patsy had finished, Carol took over. She felt the other two watching her as she climbed awkwardly into the exercise vehicle, helped by Patsy. She was going to miss her specially adapted vehicle which was so easy to get in and out of, she thought as she adjusted her reins and picked up the whip. Murray felt more like Harmony, she thought as she drove him round the manege. He was forward going and had a real air of 'look at me', yet she felt very much in control. She really enjoyed driving him, and was sad when her time was over.

Tea was followed by tack cleaning, and then there were instructional videos to watch in the evening.

"Six of us are having a go at pair driving tomorrow." Liz said later in the day.

"How do you know that?" Patsy asked.

"Ian asked if David and I would like to learn to drive a pair, and when we said yes, he said we could join you, Carol, Sadie and Jane." Liz explained. "The others are going to look round a carriage museum and a farm worked with heavy horses." Carol's heart sank. She had hoped they wouldn't be in a group with Sadie, and her pleasure at the thought of pair driving was tinged with apprehension.

CHAPTER XIV

"Where did the piebalds come from, Ian?" Sadie asked the next morning when the pair driving group had assembled. Liz and David had been given Murray and Mint to harness and drive while Sadie and Jane had two bigger 14.2hh bay ponies called Flotsam and Jetsam. Patsy had tied Paddy and Pinto up next to each other in the yard.

"They are Carol and Patsy's ponies," Ian replied. "We've had them for a week to get them started as a pair and Carol is going to learn to drive them this week." Sadie flushed with annoyance.

"I could have brought my own pair." She said to Ian angrily. He looked at her, and then said firmly.

"Your father wants you to gain experience driving different pairs. Everyone here has individual requirements and we shall try to help each one achieve those during the week," Ian paused. "Now, as you have the most experience, you and Jane can harness up and put the bays to that vehicle," he pointed to a carriage, "then when I've checked your work you can drive them down to the manege and quietly get used to them. I am going to spend a little time here before I come and see how you're getting on." Sadie looked slightly appeased.

"Right," said Ian, "Now, Liz and David, you come and watch Patsy and Carol harness up Paddy and Pinto. Then you can have a try with Murray and Mint." Sadie was quite proficient, Carol noticed, glancing sideways as the tall girl began to harness up the bays. Ian waited while she and Patsy tried to remember what to do. Carol was working from her wheelchair, handing harness to Patsy, while Ian held a pony in each hand.

"Not too bad an attempt," he said at last. "Just hold the ponies a moment Patsy, while I go and check Sadie and Jane's work and watch them put to."

"This is fun, isn't it?" David remarked. "Do you think we could start on Murray and Mint?"

"I don't see why not," Liz replied. "Carol and Patsy can tell us, and then Ian can explain where we've gone wrong!" By the time Sadie had driven out of the yard towards the manege, with Alison following, Murray and Mint were nearly ready.

"Well tried!" Ian exclaimed. He altered a few strap lengths explaining as he went. "Now, you hold your greys and watch carefully while Carol and Patsy talk their way through putting to." Alison appeared back in the yard.

"Sadie and Jane are fine, Ian," she said. "Shall I go with Carol and Patsy?"

"Yes, please, we'll join you in a few minutes."

Carol felt quite nervous as she drove into the manege. Flotsam and Jetsam looked very professional, she thought.

"Don't watch Sadie," Alison said quietly as Carol went rather close to the left gate post on entering the manege. "You concentrate on your pair, I've told Sadie to keep out of your way. Now, collect them up more and push Paddy up beside Pinto."

"The corners seem to come up very quickly today," Carol said. Her hands felt clumsy and awkward and she didn't feel nearly as comfortable as she had driving Paddy and Pinto a week ago. The ponies were wandering about and she saw Sadie give her a very scornful glance.

"Just calm down and work with Pinto and Paddy," Alison told her. "They are wandering because you are not being positive and they don't know where you want them to go." Carol made a big effort. She pulled the boys up, took a deep breath and started off again.

"Paddy, walk on. Pinto walk on," she said firmly. This time the ponies moved off together and Carol realised that by telling Paddy to start first he had extra time and so they had started much more evenly. She began to concentrate.

When Liz, David and Ian brought Murray and Mint along she was beginning to feel much more composed.

"This is boring, Ian," Sadie called. "I've been driving round for ages, avoiding the piebalds."

" OK Sadie, you can go out with Alison beside you and Jane on the backstep. Alison knows a nice drive to take you on, and I want you to be ready to answer questions on whip and hand signals, and the correct way to drive on the road by the time you get back. Make use of Alison, ask her questions, she's passed her level three and is very competent." Alison got onto the vehicle and Sadie swept grandly out of the manege. Ian called after her. "Don't let those ponies run on. Keep them collected and steady, you are not in a race. Don't show off, just drive safely."

The rest of the lesson went really well. Ian explained that one of the most important things a pair must learn was to stand still. He made Patsy hold the piebalds while he got Liz going with the greys. Then while Liz was practicing he came back and helped Carol. Later David drove and Liz back stepped, but Patsy flatly refused to try driving a pair.

"Ann's only just got me going with a single," she said firmly. "There's no way I'm ready to try driving two!" and Ian laughingly agreed. When they had finished Ian watched and helped while they took the ponies out of their vehicles back in the yard and unharnessed them. Carol couldn't do much so Ian made her instruct the others and he helped Patsy in her place. They were putting the ponies away when Sadie came back. Alison was looking rather stern. Ian turned to Carol, now in her wheelchair.

"Tell the others that you are all to come to the manege. You can learn a great deal from watching someone else's lesson." Ian was very strict with Sadie. He let her drive for a few minutes and then corrected her on several small points before asking how much of the drive Jane had driven. Jane, a quiet girl, looked startled.

"Oh I haven't driven today," she said in a surprised voice.

"That was selfish of you, Sadie," Ian remarked. "Never mind, Jane, we have finished for now, but next time Sadie will backstep for you for the whole lesson." Jane looked apprehensive, and Sadie furious, but before she had time to say anything, Ian was quizzing them on road safety. Patsy and Carol did well here, as they had spent hours practicing for the road safety competition at the Windsor Horse Show a few years ago.

When the bays had been dealt with and turned out, Ian took the six back to the house for hot soup and sandwiches. After lunch they harnessed up singles to go scurry driving.

"I've brought a strap that Dad has made for Carol, like a marathon strap." David showed it to Ian. "When we played at cones before, Carol's lack of power in her legs meant she couldn't brace her feet and she got thrown about. Can we try this?" Ian nodded.

"It sounds like a good idea to me." He helped adjust the strap. Carol and Patsy didn't change round, but the other four all took it in turns to drive or backstep.

"This is brilliant! It's much easier for me," Carol said enthusiastically to Patsy after a nippy clear round driving Mint. They were using Murray, Mint, and Magic the small black mare, because they were all about the same size. It was great fun. Ian made them change ponies and each one was slightly different to drive.

When the others got back from their outing Jacob came and found Carol.

"We've had an interesting day," he said. "How did the pair driving go?"

"I was awful to start with," Carol said ruefully, "but by the end of the lesson I felt much more in control."

"It was great fun," Liz's eyes sparkled, "David and I had Murray and Mint and they were super." Patsy had gone across to chat to some of the others and Liz and David drifted away.

"Oh, good," Jacob looked pleased. "We've got about half an hour free. I want to tell you about my idea. Let's go down by the manege for a moment." Carol wheeled her chair beside him as he walked away from the others.

"What's this all about, Jacob?" she asked.

"It's the disco on Saturday night," he said. "I thought you might feel a bit left out in a wheelchair."

"Yes," Carol said sadly. "I'm not looking forward to it. I can't use crutches, or my chair, so I shall just have to sit and watch."

"I think you can use your chair," Jacob looked at her. "I saw a programme on the wheelchair Olympics on TV some time ago. There was a disco, and some of them were making their wheelchairs whiz about in time to the music, and do all sorts of things, like wheelies. It looked quite spectacular. I thought if we practiced and kept it a secret we could surprise everyone." Carol's face brightened.

"That would be fun," she said slowly. "I'd love to be able to take part. Where could we practice?"

"What about the old corn barn? That's where they are going to have the disco. It's got a fairly level concrete floor. I went and had a look when I heard Ann and Ian talking about it."

"I think I shall have to tell Patsy. Would you mind? She'd be really upset if I left her out. We always do things together, and I

74

couldn't have managed at camp without her."

"Of course I don't mind. I knew you'd want to include her."

Carol turned impulsively to Jacob, "It's a great idea. Thanks for thinking of me." Jacob's face went red.

"That's O.K." he muttered, looking embarrassed. "We'd better get back now, but we could have our first try tomorrow about the same time again, and meet in the barn." As they made their way back Carol turned to Jacob.

"You haven't told me how your father is getting on." Jacob's face lit up.

"He's much better," he said happily, "My mother thinks he will be out of hospital next week. It will be a long time before he's fit again, but at least he'll be at home."

"Where have you been?" Patsy demanded. "I've been looking for you everywhere." Carol laughed.

"I'll tell you, but you mustn't tell anyone else."

"Not even Liz and David?" Patsy queried.

"Not yet," and Carol told her of Jacob's idea.

"He likes you," Patsy remarked casually, "he's often watching you when you don't think he is." Carol went pink.

"Don't be silly," she said crossly, and Patsy laughed.

CHAPTER XV

The days flew by and every day Carol and Patsy took out their pair, Carol gained in confidence. The two ponies had settled so that it seemed they had been driven together for ages. Patsy, Jacob and Carol managed to meet each day in the barn and practice with Carol's wheelchair, despite the fact that Ian and Ann filled nearly every hour with practical driving or stable management.

Two BDS examiners were coming on the Friday to test those who were keen take their exams. Liz was working hard on her pair driving but it was a big jump up from level two to level three and she just wasn't going to be ready. Carol felt she could take level one with some confidence, but level two was still a question mark.

"Have a go at both," Ann told her. "If you pass one and fail two you will have achieved the first step, and lost nothing. You can take level two again another time." Sadie was taking level two, but David, Patsy and Jacob weren't interested in taking any exams.

Friday morning came all too quickly for Carol.

"I feel dreadfully nervous," she confided to Patsy at breakfast. "I'm not very hungry."

"You'll be fine." Patsy looked at her friend. "What I can't understand is why you put yourself through all this agony. It will be a good thing when the exams are over. Anyway you've got me to help you."

"Have you got Mr. Whitaker or Mrs. Smythe-Browne as your examiner?" Sadie leaned across the table towards Carol. "Mr. Whitaker's a dead cinch, but Mrs. S.B. is known to be very strict. She won't like the fact that you're disabled." Carol's heart dropped. She had Mrs. Smythe-Browne.

When she was called into the tack room to do the theory part of the exam she was sure the large forbidding lady awaiting her must be able to hear the pounding of her heart. After the introductions had been made Mrs. S.B. looked at Carol.

"It's most irregular for someone disabled to attempt the exams for the able-bodied rather than those for the disabled. However I shall make no concessions, except that your groom may do the harnessing up work for you, but she may only carry out your exact instructions. We will start now with the assembly of a set of single harness. As you put it together I want you to tell me what you are doing, and what it is used for."

Carol looked at the heap of brown leather harness in pieces on the table. She picked up the parts to assemble the bridle and her hands were shaking. This is ridiculous, she thought to herself, I do this at home every day. I know I can do this. She started discussing the use of the Liverpool bit and her voice gained in confidence as she got going. Mrs. S.B. smiled when she had finished.

"That wasn't too difficult for you, was it?" she said. "Now we will discuss general stable management, ailments and shoeing." Once or twice Carol faltered. She just couldn't think of three boiled feeds and only managed linseed and barley. She had some poisonous plants to identify. Ragwort and Yew were easy, but she had never seen one of the other plants before.

"Right," Mrs. S.B. said eventually, "we'll go and find your groom, and harness up your pony." Carol wheeled her chair, with the crutches strapped on the back, and they moved out to the stable yard where Patsy was waiting with Pinto. They had decided to use Pinto because Carol had driven him so much more than Paddy. She and Patsy normally harnessed up in such a regular routine that they didn't even discuss it. Before the exam they had talked about it so Carol knew exactly what to tell Patsy to do and it worked well for them. When Pinto was harnessed up Carol got out of her wheelchair and on to crutches. Then she held Pinto and told Patsy how to put to, balancing carefully on one crutch. It was a familiar procedure. Once the vehicle was in place and everything attached correctly, Patsy replaced Carol holding Pinto and Carol moved slowly across, put her crutches into the vehicle, tucked her apron over her arm and clambered slowly into the driving seat. She pushed her crutches under the seat, adjusted her reins and whip and looked over to Mrs. S.B. who said.

"First I would like you to drive down to the manege." Carol nodded and looked at Patsy.

"Thank you," she said politely and as Patsy let go of Pinto's head, continued with "Pinto, walk on." Patsy ran round and hopped onto the backstep. After ten minutes of following instructions in the manege Mrs. Smythe-Browne told Patsy to get down and swung herself onto the back step. Carol had to ask Patsy to rebalance the exercise cart and then she took Mrs. S.B. for a drive.

During the drive the questioning continued on first aid, fire safety precautions and the highway code. Carol drove on auto-pilot, her brain worrying and puzzling over the answers she should give. At last they returned to the stable yard, and Patsy ran to Pinto's head. Mrs. S.B. got down and stood back to watch as Carol got herself and her crutches out of the vehicle and returned to her wheelchair. This time she held Pinto from her chair as she and Patsy followed their routine to take him out of the vehicle and unharness him. Patsy then led the little piebald back to the field. Mrs. S.B. looked at Carol.

"You are lucky to have such an excellent pony and such a loyal friend." Her face broke into a smile. "Congratulation on all that you have achieved. I shall pass you for both level one and level two, but your theoretical knowledge needs working on. I have been impressed by your driving ability and the way you have adapted to cope safely with your disabilities. I have to tell you that if you contemplate attempting the level three examination you will have to put in a lot more work. It is an advanced level and although your driving standard is high, you need a lot more experience outside your home environment which you might find hard to obtain." As soon as her large figure had disappeared Patsy came round the corner.

"Well?" she asked.

"I've passed both!" Carol was ecstatic. "I can't believe it. Thanks for all your help, Patsy. I'd never have even attempted the exams without you." The two girls went back towards the barns. Liz, David and Jacob pounced on Carol and Patsy as soon as they got back.

"How did you get on?" they chorused and crowded round Carol's chair. When the initial excitement had died down, Liz announced some startling news.

"Sadie's left!"

"What! You don't mean that?" Carol was amazed, "why?" she asked incredulously.

"Can't you guess?"

"She didn't fail her level two?" Patsy asked and Liz nodded. "Well, good riddance to her. We shan't miss her."

"She had a real tantrum and shouted at Ann that her examiner hadn't been fair, 'phoned her parents, packed her bags and left."

CHAPTER XVI

"Carol, Patsy, Liz and David are going to do a display on Sunday for the visiting parents driving the two pairs." Ian announced to all the children on Saturday morning. "Helen, Andrew, Jacob and Melanie, Jane and Samantha can have a scurry competition." Ann carried on.

"Your parents and friends are coming after lunch at two o'clock, so there will be plenty of time for you all to get organised, have a dress rehearsal and pack all your things on Sunday morning. Today Ian is going to take the four doing pairs driving, and I'll take the scurry drivers. After lunch all the harness will be cleaned for tomorrow." There was a general groan from them all, but Ann went on, "then you can all help get the barn ready for the disco."

Carol, Patsy, Liz and David got Pinto and Paddy and Murray and Mint harnessed up and put to. Ian asked them to drive down to the manege. To their surprise he had fitted up speakers and a tape recorder by the school. It was tremendous fun. They were all surprised how difficult it was to keep level with each other down the sides of the manege, and to change pace at exactly the same time. The music was chirpy and fitted in well with the ponies paces. By the end of an hour they felt they were beginning to put a programme together.

"Right," Ian said, "we'll stop while it's going well and have a final polishing session in the morning."

"We'll never be good enough with only one more practice!" Patsy was horrified.

"Can't we have another go this afternoon?" David asked hopefully. "I think we need it." Ian was adamant.

"No, there is enough to do this afternoon, and it's much better if the ponies don't learn to anticipate. You can go and practice on your feet in the manege if you want. You'll learn the routine much better that way."

Decorating the barn for the disco was great fun after the chore of harness cleaning was over. They cut and carried leafy branches from the wood, and Carol sat in her wheelchair in the barn blowing up endless balloons with a pump.

Tea was very frugal and Ann laughed at their faces when they saw what had been put out for them.

"You are having a good supper at the disco," she said. "I want you to work up a good appetite because we're going to have a barbeque. I don't want any rolls, sausages, burgers or chicken drumsticks left or you'll have to eat them up for breakfast!"

"That's cruel!" Andrew, who was rather plump and enjoyed his food, eyed the small plate of sandwiches with dismay. "We've been working jolly hard. How many sandwiches do we get?"

"Two each," Ann said firmly.

Later on while they were getting ready, Patsy looked at Carol in horror.

"You're not wearing a skirt!" she cried. "I'm going in jeans."

"O.K." Carol replied, "you go in jeans, I expect most of the girls will, but I'm wearing a skirt." She pulled the band off her pony tail and brushed her fair hair so it shone and fell round her shoulders. She and Jacob had practiced with her wheelchair every day in the barn, but she needed to feel she looked good to give herself confidence. The others might think she was showing off, and it might not work, but all she really wanted was to be able to join in. Liz came across. "That looks nice, Carol," she said. Carol's jaw had dropped. Liz was wearing quite a mini skirt, and suddenly she looked very grown up. "What are you staring at?" she asked Carol. "Are you ready to go over?

"Yes," Carol replied. "Come on, Patsy," she called. "We're ready to go."

As they came out of the barn David and Jacob appeared from across the yard. Carol couldn't believe her eyes. Jacob, who was so quiet, was wearing the brightest, loudest shirt she'd seen. David was much more conventional in a tee shirt and jeans.

"Who are you trying to frighten away, Jacob?" Patsy asked cheekily. "I'll need sunglasses to dance with you."

"Perhaps I shan't ask you then," Jacob retorted.

They hadn't seen the barn since tea time and the disco had been set up in a corner. Already the lights were flashing and the music blaring out. There was also an appetizing smell of food being grilled. Liz looked worried.

"What's up?" David asked her.

"I've just realised it isn't going to be easy for Carol watching

81

all of us dance," she said as they went into the barn.

"I don't think you'll have to worry, look at them!" David said in amazement. Carol, Patsy and Jacob had gone straight onto the floor and Carol was whizzing her wheelchair about while the other two danced round her.

"Hey, Carol!" David went over pulling Liz along by the hand. "That's great, who taught you to do that?" Carol grinned happily at him.

"It was Jacob's idea," she replied, as David and Liz joined them on the floor.

At some stage in the evening everybody danced along beside Carol and her chair, but even she was outshone by Jacob. He really could move to the rhythm and was quite something to watch. The evening was an enormous success.

"I've eaten too much," Patsy complained as she made an untidy heap of her clothes and clambered into her sleeping bag. "But it was a fab rave, wasn't it?"

Carol nodded. It wasn't her feet and legs that ached this time, it was her arms that were tired, but she didn't care, she had been able to join in. Who would have thought a few weeks ago that the queer, quiet boy they had met the first time they came to the driving centre could have transformed into the best dancer of the evening. What was more he had danced almost the whole evening with her, and it had been fun.

Mr. and Mrs. Lane drove their horsebox into the carriage driving centre just before two o'clock on Sunday afternoon.

"I wonder how they have got on?" Mrs. Lane said as they parked the box. She looked round to see if Carol was about. "It has been quiet without her, and without the ponies," she remarked, "I hope Carol has enjoyed it all."

Carol was busy helping Patsy harness up Pinto and Paddy.

"Look!" Liz called across to them. "Your parents have arrived." Carol turned and waved.

"Lots of people keep coming in," she said, "we're going to have quite a crowd watching us." She felt the familiar quiver of nervous excitement start in her stomach.

"You all look very busy." David's parents appeared in the yard. "What are you going to show us this time, David?" his mother asked.

"We are doing a pairs-to-music demonstration," David replied, "but we haven't had much time to practice, so don't expect anything too high powered. It was much easier doing the scurry competition at the last camp." His father laughed.

"It sounds as if you're making excuses before you've started!" He waved at the girls and smiled. "We're going to find seats. Good luck, all of you."

"Come on, you four, the seats are nearly full. You should be ready by now." Ian checked round the harness and both vehicles. "Everything looks fine. I'm going down to the manege. I want you there in five minutes."

"Help!" Liz exclaimed, pushing her hand through her copper curls. "Where on earth did I put my hat?"

"That's mine!" Patsy made a lunge for her hat before Liz could take it. "Yours is over there." She pointed behind Liz.

"Stop panicking!" David said, "They can't very well start without us, and it's no good driving down there all red faced and flustered."

They got themselves organised and made their way to the manege. They could hear Ian talking on his hand microphone.

"Right," David took command. "You know how we start. Liz and I drive right-handed to the top of the school, and you two drive left-handed to the top. Then we turn and go down the centre line side by side to X, stop and salute. Ian will start the music and we will begin our programme. Good luck!" He smiled at Carol and Liz and they entered the manege.

Ann had kitted them out in Magpie Driving Centre black and white sweat shirts with black and white quartered silks for their hard hats. They were all wearing black jodhpurs but Carol and Liz had black cotton driving aprons over theirs. They looked very smart in their matching outfits.

Liz looked across and pushed Murray and Mint on to keep parallel with the piebalds. The two vehicles turned together at the top and the four ponies were level as they pulled up to make their salute. The music started and the ponies set off in working trot. Carol was concentrating hard. It was difficult to keep level with the other pair and try to change pace at exactly the same moment. The music had a good rhythm, and the changes from walk to trot were very obvious, which made it easy for the drivers but also made any errors show up to the audience. Their performance was lively and entertaining and the crowd loved it. It was over so quickly Carol couldn't believe it as she pulled the piebalds up, next to Murray and Mint back at the centre of the school. She and Liz raised their whips and dropped their heads in salute and made their way out to the heady sound of applause.

"It went so fast!" Liz echoed Carol's sentiments as they unharnessed the ponies. "Was it O.K. Patsy? What did you think?"

"I thought it was pretty good." Patsy said smugly as she removed Paddy's bridle.

"Well, we only made a few small mistakes, and at least we didn't lose our way." David put a headcollar on Murray, ready to turn him out. As soon as the ponies had been dealt with, the four children went to watch the scurry competition, still taking place. Ian had got the audience cheering for their favourites and the atmosphere was electric. Carol leaned forward in her chair.

"Come on Jacob. Come on Melanie!" she yelled. "Get a move on!" It was no good. Helen and Andrew won by four seconds from Jacob and Melanie, with Jane and Samantha third. While they returned their ponies and vehicles to the yard the manege was set up for the prize giving.

Ian and Ann stood behind a table laden with rosettes and awards. Ann welcomed everybody and went on "I am going to start by giving prizes for the this afternoon's performances, beginning with the pairs-to-music. I would ask Liz and David, Carol and Patsy to come and collect their rosettes. I must tell you that at the beginning of the week Liz and David had never driven a pair before, and Carol and Palsy's ponies have only been driven together for a fortnight. I think you will agree their pair drive to music was very impressive. Congratulations to all four of you."

Patsy had helped Carol into her wheelchair as the crutches would be difficult in the manege. The four of them made their way to the table and Patsy gave Carol a glance as they received lovely double tiered gold rosettes. Ian motioned the four to stand still and picking up the microphone he said.

"You will now have noticed that Carol, in the wheelchair, is obviously disabled. Ann and I took her for this camp because she has worked very hard to accept her disability and she drives to a very high standard. We admire her for this, but today we are going to make a special award, not to Carol, but to the person without whom Carol simply could not drive at all. Carol doesn't know about this but we know she will be delighted as we ask Patsy to step forward to receive this special prize for her help in the background, working as Carol's groom and team mate."

Carol's eyes shone, and she clapped madly as Patsy, looking completely stunned and for once without words, went up to collect her award.

Liz and David bettered their result from the previous camp by becoming the best pair of the week, and Jacob was amazed to win a prize for the most improved whip. His mother had managed to come to watch him, so he felt very proud. He was looking forward to introducing his mother to Carol later on.

Ann took over the microphone again to announce to the audience the results from the BDS examination day. She explained that their certificates hadn't yet arrived and would be sent on to the recipients in due course. Carol could see her parents were smiling as her passes in Levels one and two were read out. Ann ended up by asking everyone to congregate in the big barn for tea.

"Ian and I have enjoyed having this group of youngsters and we hope they have all felt the week was fun and worthwhile."

David led the cheering before they all went off for tea. As they made their way Patsy turned to Carol.

"You see," she said, "gold rosettes for the pairs. Mrs. Smith was right, wasn't she? One for silver, two for gold and joy follows sorrow. It has all come true after all." The two girls smiled at each other happily as they went off to join the others and have tea.

85